A Candlelight Ecstasy Romance®

"WHO *ARE* YOU?" SHE DEMANDED. "AND WHERE ARE YOU GOING TO GET EIGHT THOUSAND DOLLARS TO LEND ME?"

Kane laughed. "Martine," he said, catching her shoulders and staring down into her eyes, "I'm somebody who wants to help you out. I swear to you, the money is mine. I'll lend it to you, and you'll sign a note to me."

She looked at him skeptically. "Wait just a minute, you mean to tell me that you just rode in like the cavalry to rescue a damsel in distress and will give me a loan with no strings attached?"

"No," he said simply. "I want to lend you the money because . . ." He paused as if searching for the right word, then said softly, "Because you fascinate me. . . ."

THE MAVERICK
AND THE LADY

Heather Graham

A CANDLELIGHT ECSTASY ROMANCE®

Published by
Dell Publishing Co., Inc.
1 Dag Hammarskjold Plaza
New York, New York 10017

For Marion Rosello, with lots of love

Dell ® TM 681510, Dell Publishing Co., Inc.

Candlelight Ecstasy Romance®, 1,203,540, is a registered trademark of Dell Publishing Co., Inc., New York, New York.

ISBN: 0-440-15207-0

Printed in the United States of America

August 1986

10 9 8 7 6 5 4 3 2 1

WFH

To Our Readers:

We have been delighted with your enthusiastic response to Candlelight Ecstasy Romances®, and we thank you for the interest you have shown in this exciting series.

In the upcoming months we will continue to present the distinctive, sensuous love stories you have come to expect only from Ecstasy. We look forward to bringing you many more books from your favorite authors and also the very finest work from new authors of contemporary romantic fiction.

As always, we are striving to present the unique, absorbing love stories that you enjoy most—books that are more than ordinary romance. Your suggestions and comments are always welcome. Please write to us at the address below.

Sincerely,

The Editors
Candlelight Romances
1 Dag Hammarskjold Plaza
New York, New York 10017

THE MAVERICK AND THE LADY

The breeze picked up suddenly, lifting a piece of tumbleweed and bouncing it forlornly across the dusty lane. The sun was just up, and the landscape was bathed in gentle mauves and golds—a lie, for the land here was anything but gentle. In the distance a rooster crowed, welcoming the morning. The sun, battling the last vestiges of night, suddenly sent its brilliant rays hurtling across the land, and Martine Galway lifted a hand to her forehead, shielding her eyes from the sudden brightness.

There was, as she had expected, a Land-Rover coming up the lane to the house. She had known Ken Lander wouldn't give her a moment's grace, just as he had known she could never repay the loan he had given her within the time specified by the promissory note.

Gritting her teeth together, Martie planted her thumbs in her jeans pockets and wedged her heels more firmly into the dirt beneath them. For one quick moment she wondered why it mattered. The Four-Leaf Clover had never been much but dust and tumbleweed.

She closed her eyes. It mattered because it was home. It mattered because Galways had been fighting for a living off the land since the potato famine had forced them from Ireland more than a century ago. It mattered because she had fought the damn land herself and because she couldn't bear to lose—especially to Ken Lander.

The silver Land-Rover was getting closer, spitting up

9

dust as it came. It would take another minute for Lander to reach the house. Martie allowed her gaze to wander. To the left of the house was a field, at long last filled with high grasses. The horses, unaware that the day had broken in doom, seemed filled with spirit this morning. Clare, a peppery red mare, nipped her colt, tossed her tail high, and went cantering along the fence in freedom. Martie envied the horse.

She squared her shoulders and gazed down the lane once more. The Land-Rover was still coming, jolting in a way that for once made Martie grateful that the long drive was filled with potholes.

God, but it was a comedy! she thought bitterly. *The Perils of Pauline.* Any minute now he would come and tell her he owned the place.

Tears sprang to her eyes, but she would not let them fall and blinked against them. There was one out. And in the end, she wondered, would it matter if she took that way?

The sun rose higher. Once again she lifted a hand to shield her eyes from its glare. Staring past the fields and the approaching vehicle, she frowned. High up on the western ridge she could see a single horseman. He was just poised there, very still, and it seemed that he was looking down at the ranch. Who the hell was it? she wondered. The neighboring ranchers should be busy with their chores. And she had never seen the horse before. It was a magnificent creature, a good seventeen hands, sleek and beautiful against the changing panorama of the sky.

Martie sighed. She had her own problems to deal with that morning.

The Land-Rover pulled up in front of her, spewing dust. Martie didn't step back; she just closed her eyes for a moment as the dust settled over her. The door of the Land-Rover opened, and Ken Lander stepped out.

He was a tall man, blond and handsome—or he would

10

be handsome, she thought, if there weren't a look about his eyes that hinted of cruelty, a love of power, and the need to bring others low. He did have a certain power; of that Martie was well aware. Even as a child he'd been ruthless; even in his teens he'd attracted women, used them. But something about the coldness in his blue eyes had always made Martie want to squirm. Maybe because she knew all too well the way he'd managed to discard Susan Riley—among others.

He took a step toward her, his bronzed face creased with a smile of triumph. Her heart fluttered furiously once, and then the calm she had assumed returned to her. She glanced too quickly over his pristine form; for a rancher, Ken managed to stay too damned clean. From his tan suede jacket to his snakeskin boots, he looked like the upwardly mobile man-about-town, ready to make his mark on the world. Well, she couldn't accuse him of being stupid. He'd made half the valley his—and more than half the people in it. And he was trying to do the same to her today.

"Morning, Martine," he said, pausing at the hood of the Land-Rover to lean casually against it. The gesture was obvious. She was going to come to him, crawl to him if he had his way. "I see you were expecting me."

"Kenneth," she replied, hooking both thumbs into her jeans pockets again. "Yes, I was expecting you." The breeze picked up again and lifted her hair, sent it flying about her shoulders and throat, catching the rising sun, and gleaming with touches of deep fire.

She wished suddenly that she'd had the sense to tie it up that morning. Ken's hand twitched, his grin deepened, and she knew that he was thinking he'd like to tangle his fingers in it.

She felt a little ill, but she couldn't show it.

"Well?" he asked, apparently growing impatient.

"Well what?" she demanded.

"Have you got the money?"

"You know damned well I haven't. Not the full amount."

"Well, well, well . . ."

He reached into his jacket pocket and pulled out a slim cigar. He studied it for a moment before flicking his monogrammed lighter. "What are we going to do about this sad state of affairs?"

What are we going to do? The question reverberated in her mind. She swallowed fiercely, hoping he didn't see the small gesture. Would she be a fool to think a moment's loss of virtue worth the ranch, worth a hundred years of struggle?

"Martine?"

"I have half the money," she said.

"Half? Not good enough."

"If I had just another week or two—"

"Martine, Martine!" Lander puffed on his cigar and watched the smoke fade away. Then he smiled at her, and she felt herself tremble a little because the slight motion of his mouth was such a sexual threat. "You knew the terms when you signed those papers. Today the principal is due in full or else I take the ranch. Unless, of course, you can find something to say—or do—to convince me to extend the loan."

"Like what?" Martine asked, hedging.

"I think we both know the answer to that, don't we?"

"Why are you doing this?" she inquired quietly, wondering if it was possible to appeal to decency in him—if there was any decency in him.

"Why?" he repeated softly. "Come on over here, Martine, and I'll try to tell you about it."

Take the step, and damn foolish pride, she thought. Maybe there was still a chance. If she could just be a little cajoling, she might trick him into a little time.

She wanted to lower her eyes; she didn't allow herself.

Keeping her thumbs rigidly in her pockets, she started to walk, meeting his mocking gaze steadily. For a moment she hated herself. And then she, too, mocked Martine Galway in her thoughts. What had she been expecting this morning? This was no longer the great Wild West. The days of gun battles were over. The cavalry was not going to ride to the rescue. She knew her choices: Give him the ranch—or herself.

She stopped about a foot in front of him, and her chin naturally raised. She was a slim five-five, and at an inch or so more than six feet, plus his boots, he towered over her.

He reached out to catch a stray tendril of her hair; her jaw locked hard so she wouldn't flinch, but he saw the gesture and smiled. "Still think you're too good for me, Martie?"

"I never thought I was too good for you, Ken," she replied levelly, meeting his eyes.

"Yes, you did. You were always Pat Galway's daughter, the town aristocracy! Cheerleader, prom queen . . ."

"Come on, Ken. We haven't been children for a decade—"

"Maybe it wasn't always your fault," he interrupted. "Ever since your grandfather married that French woman, the Galways thought they were breeding something special. That's when they became so damned arrogant."

His finger had strayed from her hair to her cheek, from her cheek to her throat, and now hovered over the rise of her breasts. She pushed it aside.

"We didn't become arrogant with my grandmother. The Galways have always had a penchant for recognizing trash—and dealing with it accordingly."

"Why, you uppity little bitch!" he snapped, his smile disappearing from his face. Martie worried that she had

13

gone too far; she took another step back and then another as he stalked her.

"Get away from me, Ken Lander!" she exclaimed furiously. "You can take the ranch, but you can't take me!"

"Can't I? You know, I think that's the trouble with you, Martine Galway. You've wanted someone to take you for a long, long time. You've been getting pruned and soured up here, a woman all alone. And you know what else, Martine?"

"I don't want to know anything!" she told him, growing alarmed at the tic of anger in his cheek, at the way his fists were clenched at his side. She didn't trust him. She knew he'd hurt a number of people before, yet she hadn't believed he'd dare attack her on her property in broad daylight. "And I'm not alone here," she cried out more defensively than she wanted to. "I've got ranch hands—"

"Who all are miles away, working, aren't they?"

He caught her wrists. She struggled furiously with him, kicking and scratching. "I don't mind a little tussle," he told her.

"Damn you! Let me go. So help me God, I'll bring charges—"

"Charges?" His query was so polite that she paused, and as she did so he caught her ankle with his foot, sending her sprawling to the ground. The dust and dirt filled her mouth, and she coughed as she tried desperately to roll away. But then he was down on her, straddling her waist, catching her wrists.

When she met his eyes again, she didn't like what she saw at all. He wanted revenge—for whatever supposed wrongs all the Galways had done to him. She stilled, thinking her only chance would be to catch him off guard.

"Charges? I don't think so, Martine. If you bring charges, I'll just have to be real embarrassed. I wouldn't want to have to say the things about a lady that I'd have

14

to say about you. Remember, you did sign the note. I just came over to see about my investment. And there you were, trying to bribe your way out of debt with your body."

"Who would believe you?"

"A lot of people know you'd sell your soul to save the ranch. I'd never deny having you, honey, just your reception to the situation. And like I said, Martine, I think that line's comparable to all the manure in the valley. You've been asking for it for a long, long time."

His hold on her wrist was going lax. With a wild burst of energy and fury she freed her hand and brought her nails against his cheek. He swore and tightened his knee grip around her waist. He touched the blood on his cheek briefly, then easily caught her fists. Martine gasped with dismay as her shirt gave in the struggle, the buttons ripping off the faded blue denim and the material falling away. She was heaving with exertion, and above the low-cut lace of her bra the mounds of her breasts rose and fell furiously, drawing his amused gaze when he at last subdued her. She tensed as his face came close to hers, grinding her teeth together hard against the strong, handsome features ruined by the look of absolute ruthlessness.

"You'll pay for this!" she growled. "I'll scream—"

"And who will hear you—except the tumbleweed?" he said mockingly. Then he laughed. "Trust me, Martie, in seconds I'll have you screaming with pleasure."

"I swear I'll—"

"Always the fighter, Martie. You know, that's one thing I like about you. But I like a lot about you. I've always liked to watch you move, honey. You've got a body that doesn't quit. You know, Martine, I could probably even be persuaded to marry you."

"Marry! You're insane—"

"No," he drawled quietly. "This seems just right to me. Maybe it's the way I always wanted you. Martine

15

Galway, naked in the dirt. Taken in the dirt by a man who knows just how to handle her. You're going to discover that you just love it."

He straightened to strip away his suede jacket, and she made another wild bid for freedom, unable to believe what was happening. For all her struggles, for all her bitter fight, she was about to be raped in the dirt by an egoist convinced it was what she wanted.

And she couldn't stop it. She was sobbing and striking at him furiously, but he was stronger and just kept laughing. He tossed her back to the dirt so hard that she was stunned, and in the daze in which she now fought she saw him stand. He gripped his belt buckle, getting ready to come down to her again. She closed her eyes and started to scream.

But she was interrupted by a sound, something she barely heard against her own scream. It was a strange whisper, like a furious breeze that ripped through the air; it was followed by a thunk—and Lander's startled gasp.

Martie opened her eyes with amazement. Ken Lander was lying on the ground a few feet away from her, arms and torso entangled in a perfect lasso. He was cursing away and fighting the rope, but it was only being jerked more tightly around him.

Martie looked up.

There was the horse—the horse she had seen on the ridge—and beyond the horse stood a man.

Dazed as she was, she could barely make out his features. He was tall and lean but apparently muscular beneath the faded blue of his work shirt and jeans. Blinking against the sun, she at last began to see his face beneath the shade of his low-brimmed hat. His eyes were gleaming and bright against the rugged bronzed contours of his hard-set features. His uncompromising jaw was twisted in anger that was reflected in the hazel gleam of his tawny gold eyes. He was not as handsome as Ken, but he

16

was arresting. He glanced her way but said nothing. Nor did he help her to her feet. He pulled at the end of the rope he held, drawing Ken Lander to his feet.

"Who the hell do you think you are?" Ken raged, struggling with the rope, despising the humiliation he felt as he rose. "This is a private affair—"

"It isn't any affair at all, as far as I can see," the stranger interrupted coolly. His voice was rich, a baritone in keeping with the rough landscape around them.

"Listen, drifter," Ken growled, struggling with the rope, "you don't know who I am in this town. You're going to rue the day you were born when I finish with you—"

"You'll rue the fact that you were born at all if you don't remove your carcass from this property—quickly," the unperturbed stranger drawled threateningly.

"Let go of that rope!" Lander shouted.

The stranger did so with a shrug. Ken freed himself, then charged the man. Martie barely saw what happened. The stranger stood still and raised a fist. There was a resounding crunch, and then Lander was on the ground.

"Get out of here," the man said with disgust.

Warily wiping a trickle of blood from his mouth, Lander rose, his eyes on the man. "You ass, it's my property now."

"Not until midnight. And until then I'm telling you—get off this land!" His voice barely rose, but the warning was unmistakable.

Ken grabbed his hat from the dirt and dusted it off against his jeans. He gave Martine a look of pure venom. "You'll get yours, baby, trust me. There's nothing that can save you now."

"Go!" the stranger commanded.

Ken Lander got into the Land-Rover. The engine revved like an enraged cat, and dirt flew and spewed from underneath the tires as he drove away.

Still stunned, Martie stared up at the horseman who had—as ridiculous as it might seem—ridden down from the ridge to save her in the nick of time.

A slight grin touched his features as he stared at her, twitching the corners of his mouth. He watched her while he began to rewind his rope. She wondered why he did not come to help her to her feet, then realized that her shirt was half open. She nervously clutched at the edges to bring it together. She should be thanking him, but she couldn't find anything to say—at least not while his keen gaze was touching her with golden sparks.

"Thank you," she said at last.

"You're welcome."

She tried to sit while holding her shirt at the same time.

"If you think I'm going to help you up, Ms. Galway, don't. No assistance in the world is any good unless it's given to someone with the courage to rise out of the dirt alone."

Her cheeks flamed brightly, and forcing her muscles to move, she rose with what she thought was a fair amount of grace for the situation.

"Who are you?" she demanded.

He shrugged. "No one, really. My name is Kane Montgomery. Since you seem to have some free time now, thanks to me, I'd like a cup of coffee. And maybe some bacon and eggs."

"I—of course," Martie murmured, grateful, of course, but also thoroughly disturbed by his presence.

Still clutching her shirt, she started for the house. She could barely hear his footsteps behind her, but she could feel him, radiating a heat more intense than the sun.

Who the hell, she wondered, was Kane Montgomery?

CHAPTER ONE

Martie pushed open the screen door to the house. When she heard it swing shut, she turned around, blinking against the subdued interior light. For a moment all she could see was a silhouette again: the tall man, lean and wiry—and very disturbing with his quiet air.

"There's coffee on in the kitchen," she motioned to the left of the huge parlor. "If you'll go ahead and help yourself, I'll, uh." She paused, glancing down at her ripped shirt in explanation. "I'll be right with you."

"Thank you."

He stepped past her and Martine watched his shoulders, broad and taut beneath his cotton shirt, until he disappeared past the swinging door. Then she sighed and looked about the room.

It was beautiful. The ranch house was more than a hundred years old; it had originally been built by French trappers then was refurbished as a cathouse in the gold rush days. It had maintained a stately elegance anyway, and though every generation had added on and modernized in one way or another, it was still an old-fashioned and gracious place. In the back of the house, past the French doors that led to the office and bedrooms, was a game room as vast as the parlor. From the game room the view was a very modern one. Wall-to-ceiling glass looked out onto the pool and a barbecue and patio that could accommodate several hundred guests.

If she could ever afford a hundred guests, Martine thought bitterly. Parts of the ranch might not have changed much in a century, but times certainly had for her. She sighed. Then she forced herself to forget about the house for a minute and turn down the right hallway to enter her bedroom.

In the bathroom she repeatedly splashed her face with cool water, then pressed a cold cloth to her cheeks. What had it all been for? she wondered wearily. She was grateful to Kane Montgomery—whoever he was—but what good had any of it been? She might have gained a few more hours with his help, but she had lost. Even if the ranch didn't belong to Ken Lander now, it would by tomorrow morning.

She sighed, quickly grabbed a T-shirt from her drawer and, with an oath of fury, tore her ruined shirt to shreds. She then flung it into the wastebasket.

Oh, but this whole damned thing was incredible! If only she'd been born a male. She might have lost the ranch, but she'd have never found herself in the predicament she'd been rescued from. *The Perils of Pauline* indeed!

Kane Montgomery, she reminded herself, was sitting in her kitchen. She quickly grabbed a brush to run through her tangled hair, then left her bedroom behind, surprised that she felt a little breathless, that her heart seemed to be pounding too fast.

He was there. She saw him as soon as she passed through the swinging doors. He was leaning against the counter, staring out the window to the eastern fields. She knew he heard her, but he took several seconds to leave his vigil and turn to face her. To her surprise, she found herself the object of his thorough scrutiny. His strange tawny gold eyes moved over her from head to toe, very slowly. Annoyed that a blush was rising to her cheeks, Martine hurried into the room, passing him on her way to the refrigerator. He didn't touch her, but his scent lingered, a scent of leather and horses, fresh soap and . . . something else. He wasn't wearing after-shave, but there was still something pleasant and appealing.

"Ah, you said bacon and eggs, right?" Martine inquired, reaching into the refrigerator to find the desired foodstuffs. It was just him, she realized, trembling a little. His scent . . . It was just him, very clean and very male.

"Right."

Not "Right, thank you," or "Right, if you don't mind," just "Right." Martie reached for the bread, too, and brought the things to the counter. He watched her, then left his position at the counter to sit on a chair at the kitchen table. She felt a little odd with her back to him and wondered at the wisdom of asking the man into her house. Beyond a shadow of doubt Ken Lander would have raped her. But had she been saved from a rapist only to find herself in more trouble? No, surely not! But —Kane Montgomery was dangerous. That fact, too, left no room for doubt.

"How would you like your eggs?" she asked as she turned to face him, not so much because she cared as because she wanted to see what he was doing. He was sitting, leaning back in the chair, idly smoking a cigarette while he watched her. He had taken off his hat and tossed it onto an empty chair, and she could see that his hair was Indian black, without a streak of gray. She couldn't tell if his age was closer to thirty or forty, only that it wouldn't matter to him. He seemed to consider himself a law unto himself. He probably had for quite some time. He wasn't handsome in a conventional way, but his features were fine and strong, with a fascinating appeal. To soften the hard line of his bronzed jaw, there was a small cleft in the center of his chin. He had dimples, too, when he chose to smile. His hair parted at the side but fell slightly over his forehead; she was willing to bet it an-

21

noyed him when he was busy. That sleek darkness contrasted sharply with the tawny gold brilliance of his keen eyes, making them appear like those of a cougar, always wary and dangerous.

"Scrambled will be fine," he told her. She gave him a little smile and turned back to her work, reaching over the counter for a bowl in which to scramble the eggs. The bacon she decided to stick in the microwave. She didn't ask him if he minded; she just did it, certain that he would want his bacon fried.

She jumped when he spoke again.

"Want to tell me about it?"

"What?" she asked, spinning around.

He grinned, and when he did, she saw that he had white, even teeth. And his features didn't look quite so hard or craggy; they were really very nice, just set with his own brand of determination. "I said, do you want to tell me about it? To the most undiscerning eye, Ms. Galway, this is not your usual situation. What's going on here?"

She turned back to the counter. "You mean Ken Lander?"

"If he's the pretty boy that I suggested leave your property, then, yes, I mean Ken Lander."

She looked at him again just as he was leaning across the table to crush out his cigarette in the ashtray. He had expected her to turn; his tawny eyes were sharp as he gazed at her.

She shrugged. "It's rather obvious. I was in financial trouble. The banks didn't want to touch me. He offered me a loan that I believed I could pay. . . . I couldn't."

"So he wanted his ounce of flesh?"

She was annoyed to see that one black-as-ink brow was raised at her a little skeptically. "That's the story," she answered sharply, spinning around to attack the eggs with a fork.

22

"In a nutshell anyway."

Martine turned on the gas, set the skillet on the stove, and almost sent the eggs flying out of it by tossing them in with vehemence. She didn't care. She pirouetted cleanly again and strode to the table with her hands on her hips.

"Who are you—and what is all this to you?"

He laughed, and she decided that he was closer to thirty than forty—just very, very sure of himself.

"I told you—"

"Yes, yes, that your name is Kane Montgomery. But you're asking a lot of questions for a man who seems to have tripped into being a hero, is anxious for breakfast—and nothing else."

He stood, then touched her shoulders to step past her and rescue the burning eggs. "I'm looking for a job," he told her. "I hear your foreman's laid up with a broken leg. You could use me. And since I did happen to trip into being a hero, I think that out of common courtesy you might want to offer a few explanations."

Martine dropped into the chair he had vacated, suddenly so weary and frustrated that she picked up his coffee cup and sipped it without thinking about her action. "You've really got the only explanation. I've known Ken Lander a long time. I've never trusted him; he's always resented the Galways. But I thought I could pay the loan. And I could have if my cattle hadn't gotten sick," she muttered fiercely, closing her eyes with the painful memory. It had been a strange and isolated outbreak of hoof-and-mouth disease. Isolated, of course, because between her and the government, they hadn't allowed it to spread. But it was strange because it was a viral disease that had suddenly—out of the clear blue—attacked only *her* cattle. It had been a nightmare for her, watching the cattle sicken, finding herself quarantined, discovering that a

23

good portion of the herd had to be put to death, and then working around the clock to disinfect the entire ranch.

That, at least, was in the past. Martine opened her eyes and shrugged. "I can't give you a job," she told him. Surely that had to be as obvious as everything else. "You might have bought me a few hours, but I don't own this place anymore."

The eggs were done. Without asking, he searched quickly through the cabinets and brought out two plates. Martine frowned as she followed his movement. He pulled the bacon out of the microwave next and divided the food neatly.

"I'm not hungry," she said, but the plate clattered to the table in front of her anyway.

"I've got this strange feeling you haven't eaten this morning," he told her, "and that isn't any way to run a ranch."

Martine sat back and folded her arms over her chest, smiling with exasperation. "Mr. Montgomery, you do not look at all daft, nor do you seem to be hard-of-hearing. I told you, I don't own this place anymore."

He pulled out the chair next to her and sat, pushing a fork and napkin her way. "Hey, get another cup and the coffee, will you? You drank mine."

With a vast sigh—and not at all sure whether to be angry or amused—Martine decided to comply. She poured herself a cup of coffee and refilled his.

"Have you got any juice?" he asked.

"As a matter of fact," she replied a little tersely, "I do."

She brought the juice and said sarcastically, "anything else? Champagne, caviar? I'm afraid I'm out."

His fingers wound around her wrist, and she glanced down at them. They were as bronzed as his face, as lean as his long, hard body. The nails were clipped, clean, and neat. His palm and his fingertips were calloused; they were the hands of a man accustomed to work.

But then she had known that he was accustomed to physical activity; it was in the way he moved, confident and secure at all times.

"Sit down," he said.

She pulled her hand away, staring at him a little deliberately. He was nothing but a drifter, she tried to tell herself. She would not be intimidated by him.

She sat, determined to be amused by the interlude. God knew she could use some amusement. The rest of the day promised only nightmares.

Kane Montgomery had no problem eating. He consumed half his food, then persisted with his questioning. "Tell me more about this thing between you and Lander."

Martine lifted her hands in a gesture of weary annoyance. "I've told you the whole story! It's as simple as what I said and what you saw."

Kane took a sip of his coffee, watching her over the rim of his mug. Then he said, "Lady, that man has a grudge against you, not your family. What did you do to him?"

"Me?" Martine said angrily. "I never did a damn thing to him! Ken Lander hates everyone in this valley, but no one was ever cruel to him. His father was a useless drifter, but everyone around here took Ken in when he was a boy. And then he didn't need any help. He saved up some money and started buying everything in sight—whether the owners wanted to sell or not."

Kane sat back, drumming his fingers on the table. "Sounds like he's got a bit of a social problem."

"If you want me to feel sorry for him, forget it!" Martine exclaimed. "He grew into a cruel and avaricious man. And worse." She paused, staring down at her coffee cup. "A friend of mine almost committed suicide because of him."

"Oh?"

She looked up at him. He appeared intensely interested, and she shrugged. "Her name is Susan. She was always crazy about him, and somewhere along the line he decided he wanted her. Susan was a nice kid. A little sheltered probably. Anyway, she eventually moved in with him. I don't think he actually beat her, but he tossed her around like winter wood. She stayed like a fool, because she had fallen so deeply in love with him. Then she got pregnant. He told her in no uncertain terms that he didn't want to marry her or be saddled with a child. He made the appointment and took her for the abortion." Martine paused for a minute. "She went a little crazy after that. Oh, what difference does any of this make? Tonight I'm out of here. There's nothing else left to do."

"Nothing?" His eyes mocked her. "You're not much of a fighter, are you, Ms. Galway?"

"What are you talking about?" Martine demanded angrily. "I've done everything I could. I've been to every financial institution in the damned county, tried every trick possible with the ranch. I—"

"How much do you owe, and how much do you have?"

"What the hell is it to you?" Martine said angrily.

He reached into his shirt pocket for a pack of cigarettes and took a long time lighting one. She noticed a little tic in a vein in his strong neck, and for a moment she was very nervous again. He had a temper all right; he just seemed to know how to control it. Her explosive words hung between them like tension in the air, and inwardly she trembled. Her eyes seemed drawn to his hands and on to the breadth of his chest, and then her lashes lowered because she had followed the pearl buttons of his shirt downward as his body narrowed to his waist. She was annoyed that she was swallowing and blushing again. Damn! He was a breed of man she had never met before; just being near him spoke of heat and tension, and while she wondered about him in a way that made her body grow warm, she was also warning herself that if she should make a move he didn't like, he would probably stop her with the speed and skill of an angry rattler.

"I'm sorry," she murmured at last, remembering that whoever or whatever he was, he had come from the blue to save her from what would have definitely been rape. She kept her eyes on her coffee cup and played idly with the handle. "I would have done just about anything to save this place." She looked up at last. "It means a lot to me."

He shifted slightly in his chair, stretching his long legs out, exhaling smoke and watching it rise in her sunny yellow kitchen.

"Why?"

"Because it's my home. It's my . . . heritage." She smiled a little wanly at last. "At the far end of my two hundred acres is the old town church. Both my parents are buried there." She lifted a hand to indicate the house. "This is a beautiful place. They made it that. The ranch encompasses hills and ponds and streams and can be a paradise all in itself." She smiled. "I grant you, I have dust and dirt and tumbleweed too. But"—she waved her hand again—"it has everything."

He did not follow the wave of her hand; she was certain that he didn't need to. He knew something about the ranch, and he had already ascertained that a lot of hard work had gone into it all.

"What happened to the finances?" he asked bluntly.

She paled a little. "My mother died when I was little. I barely remember her. But my father . . . died just last year. He'd had triple bypass surgery and was in the hospital for months the year before." She paused because

27

she'd be damned if she were going to cry in front of a hard, assessing stranger, even if she did feel she owed him a few explanations since he had saved her. Brusquely she added, "Insurance for independent ranchers isn't the greatest in the world. Dad had to go to a number of doctors, and it was really quite easy to eat up the savings and the income."

"I'm sure it was."

She looked up at him quickly but could fathom little from his gaze. His eyes were fascinating, she thought: fringed with thick dark lashes, searing where stars of yellow shot out from the pupils, deeper gold beyond that color, all blending to the shade of a newly washed gold nugget.

"Maybe I can help you," he told her.

She started to laugh, then realized how rude it sounded. "I'm sorry, Mr. Montgomery—"

"If I'm going to work for you," he interrupted, "you should get used to calling me Kane."

Laughter bubbled in her chest again. No, she couldn't start laughing because she'd start crying. She sobered quickly. "Kane, I owe twenty thousand dollars. I've got twelve. I just don't see—" She stopped abruptly. She had been about to tell him she couldn't see where a drifting ranch hand could come up with that kind of money. She rephrased her sentence. "I don't see how anyone could raise it."

He shrugged, and she felt uncomfortable because now his eyes did tell her something: They told her that he knew exactly what she had really been going to say.

"Your friends can't come through with that much?"

"No. Ken Lander has been trying to buy everyone out. He already has a number of politicians in his pocket," Martine said bitterly. "Seriously, in twentieth century America the entire situation is a joke. I'm probably best out of it."

28

"Then why did you meet him this morning?"

"Because I was a fool. I believed I could talk some sense into him."

His jaw twisted a little, and inky lashes shielded his gaze. Something like a hot sizzle passed between them, touching Martine to her core. She knew now what he was thinking, and she didn't like his thoughts at all. He was wondering if she hadn't somehow invited Ken Lander into the very scene that he had interrupted.

Then he voiced his thoughts. "You weren't considering a different kind of payoff to the man, were you?"

She sat still for a minute, then felt her anger rise like a rocket to dictate her actions.

"You bastard!" Martine hissed, and she was on her feet, her hand flying through the air to strike him. But he was standing, too, and she found she had been right about him: He could move with the speed and grace of a rattler. She never touched him. His fingers closed around her wrist, and she gasped a little. But then her hand was dropped, and he was moving away.

"Calm down. Just say no and I'll believe you."

"That mentality is the most infuriating—"

"I don't really know you, do I?" he drawled.

Martine braced her teeth together. "Perhaps you don't," she said at last, very coolly. But he didn't seem to notice her tone.

"Have you got that money in a checking account?" he demanded.

"What?"

"Dammit!" Kane swore, his patience seeming to wear thin. "The money you owe Lander. Can you write a check?"

"I—"

"Don't stutter. Answer me!"

"Yes, dammit, yes! What—"

"Write it out."

29

"Write it out? Are you crazy? He won't take it, and if you go anywhere near him, it's likely that you'll find yourself under lock and key."

He smiled suddenly, and she felt again that he was young, arresting in the damnedest, most disturbing way. "Aren't you willing to chance another loan?"

"What?"

"I swear, woman, I thought I'd saved a damsel with some amount of intelligence and her faculties for hearing. I asked you a question."

"I heard you," Martine retorted. "But I told you, I've been everywhere. I don't know anyone who can help."

"You know me."

"You?" she whispered. "But where—"

"Does it matter? I promise I didn't rob any banks or trains, nor am I a cattle rustler."

"I didn't say that."

"Fine. Then there's no problem. I'll lend you the eight thousand. You sign over a note to me."

"Wait a minute," Martine said a little breathlessly. "I won't—I mean, there won't be any, uh, strings attached to this thing?" Now she was blushing furiously, and she hated herself for it. Damn, she thought she'd acquired a small amount of confidence. And she had, she assured herself quickly. It had just been an unusual morning, from start to finish. And Kane Montgomery was an unusual man—to say the least. And God, after Ken, didn't she need to protect herself first?

His mouth twitched with open amusement, and his gaze raked her very slowly, very thoroughly.

"What was that, Ms. Galway?"

"I—you're going to lend me the money, just like that? No, uh, strings attached." The color had now completely fled from her face. His careful scrutiny continued. Then he met her eyes again.

"Do you mean, am I demanding that you hop into bed for a loan?"

She would have given her eyeteeth to be able to strike him. Knowing the gesture would be futile, she was glad that he stood across the room. "Well?" She challenged him coolly.

He laughed, and she felt his eyes move their disturbing golden warmth over her again. "What makes you so certain I'd want the kind of payment you're worrying about?" He taunted her with a wicked grin.

She knew that her color had brightened to a brilliant crimson, and it irritated her. She struggled to keep her tone low and aloof. "There's no catch to this? No strings attached? Why would you, a perfect stranger, want to make a loan like this?"

He paused for several moments, the play of a smile curling his lips. "I like women who can pick themselves up out of the dirt," he told her. "And like I said, I want a job. No ranch, no work."

Martine shook her head. "Why don't I believe this?"

He shrugged. "What's to worry about? Write your check out to Lander. I'll see that it's delivered." When she kept hesitating, staring at him, he asked, "What have you got to lose?"

Martine shrugged, then turned slowly to leave the kitchen. She felt his eyes on her all the way out, and once past the swinging doors she paused for a deep breath. Who was he? How had he happened to walk into her life just in the nick of time?

She gave herself a shake and hurried into her bedroom. It didn't really matter because he had made one great point: She hadn't a thing to lose by trusting him—except her $12,000, she reminded herself dryly. But he wanted the check made out to Ken Lander, and surely he wasn't a forger.

Martine decided she had to take the reckless plunge.

When she had the check written and returned to the kitchen, he was gone. A frown creased her brow as she wondered just what his game was. Then she raced quickly back through the parlor and out the front door.

He was already astride the magnificent bay. He smiled at her, reaching for the check. "You should relax a little, you know," he told her. "That's a nice pool out back. Go spend some time at it."

"I doubt if I could right now," Martine said sweetly, inclining her head toward the check in his hand. "I'm afraid I'm just not that trusting."

He grimaced but seemed not to take offense at her words. Then he stared toward the long driveway to the road, and his eyes, sharply narrowed, came back to hers. "Where are your ranch hands?" he asked.

She waved vaguely toward the east. "Fixing fences."

"On the day you were due to lose the place?"

She shrugged dryly. "Business as usual. Cattle have to be fed, Kane. And penned. If you plan on being a fore-man, you must know that."

"Oh, I do know cattle, Ms. Galway," he said lightly. His smile faded as he added sternly, "Do me a favor. Don't hang around outside until your men get back. Thor here is a bit of a wonder horse, but we can't make town and back in the twinkling of an eye."

"Thor?" Martine raised a slightly mocking eyebrow.

"I didn't name him" was all Kane said. Thor nuzzled Martine's shirt slightly, then seemed to turn of his own accord.

Standing in the dusty pathway, Martine was left to wonder when—and if—he would return. The great bay ate the dirt in great lengths with a canter as smooth as the flight of a bird, but at the highway the horse came to an abrupt halt. Kane Montgomery was looking back at her. He lifted a hand in salute and then was gone. Mar-tine stared after him for a long while before she slowly

32

returned to the house. Once there she sat down and stared out the front bay windows for a long, long time. At last she gazed down at her watch. Thank God, it was after twelve!

She leaped off the old sofa and hurried into the kitchen. Within minutes she had concocted herself a huge, peppery Bloody Mary. The celery would have to do for lunch.

Long before noon Kane Montgomery rode through the high wrought-iron gates of another ranch. A number of men were breaking a few wild mustangs as he came down the drive, and he waved to the hands, who called out greetings. Moments later he was in front of a huge, white, sprawling ranch house, one that was cool and breezy in the Mexican style. Thor's hooves clattered lightly over stones in the courtyard; then Kane dismounted from the horse and gave him a firm slap on the hindquarters. He knew Thor; the bay would head straight for the barn, and old Sam would laugh with delight, remove the horse's saddle and trappings, and probably supply him with a nice handful of the best alfalfa available.

Kane smiled as he watched the bay trot off, then entered the front door without knocking. There was no one around as he crossed over the Spanish tiles to the bar in the back of the room. He tossed his hat onto a brown leather chair, wiped his brow with his shirtsleeve, then ducked behind the bar to find the refrigerator and dig out an ice-cold beer. It was one hell of a red-hot day.

The beer went down smoothly. Nursing it along and appreciating the coldness, Kane walked back around the bar to stare out at the dome-screened pool that lay beyond open arches. One hand on his hip, the other wrapped around his beer, he stared at the tranquil setting but didn't see it. The beer had cooled him, but he had

33

grown hot all over again, thinking of the scene he had interrupted at the Four-Leaf Clover that morning.

"Martine Galway." He said her name aloud as if testing it with his tongue. He could still hear the ferocity of her voice as she had fought Lander; he could still see the brilliant blue-green blaze of her eyes as she raged against the man.

And he admitted a little wryly, he could all too clearly remember her compact form: the rise of her half-exposed breasts before she thought to grab at her shirt, the narrow enchantment of her waist, and the definite lure that was the flare of her hips.

"Kane. You beat me back!"

He turned with a slow frown at the sound of the gruff voice. The man approaching him was almost as tall as, but several decades older, than Kane was. His hair was as white as drifting snow but still thick upon his head.

For an old coot, Joe Devlin, you cut a fine figure, Kane thought, extending his hand to take the one offered him.

"Yeah, Joe," Kane said.

"Did you get out to the Four-Leaf Clover?" Joe asked anxiously.

"That I did," Kane said dryly.

"And?" Joe walked to the bar but watched Kane as he did so. Kane followed him and took a seat in one of the huge leather chairs that flanked the fireplace beyond the bar.

"I came upon the lady in question under a certain amount of duress," Kane told the older man, his eyes following Joe's movements as he also pulled out a cold beer, then took a chair opposite Kane.

Joe's thick white brows were pulled over his eyes in a worried frown. "Lord a'mighty! Was she hurt?"

"No." Kane decided not to go into detail. "But Lander was there. With a little persuasion he left."

"Did he recognize you?"

34

"No. Why should he?"

"Your picture's been around," Joe said thoughtfully, "but maybe not too much. So go on. What's the real problem?"

Kane shrugged. "Martine Galway admitted she signed a promissory note to him. And the note was due today."

"Damn!" Joe exploded. "It's my fault the fool girl ever did a thing like that to begin with."

"Your fault? How?" Kane asked. "Joe, you're a Senator. When the Senate's in session, you've got to be there."

"Not to the point that I don't know what's going on in my own backyard!" Joe distractedly drummed his fingers against the arms of the chair. "Thank God Bart got wind of this in time." He stood and angrily paced over to stare out at the pool as Kane had done. "I promised that girl's father I'd watch out for her. Some guardian I turned out to be."

"There wasn't much you could have done," Kane said. "The 'girl' is a woman, Joe. And a spitfire if I've ever seen one. You could never hover over her like a mother hen."

"Yes, but if I'd just been available, she'd have come to me for assistance."

There was no real answer for that, but Kane loved the old man, so he gave him the best assurance he could. "Joe, it doesn't matter. It's all over now. I'm going to find Lander, pay him, and see that he keeps his distance." Kane stood, finished his beer, and set the empty bottle on the bar. "Mind if I keep that bay of yours for a while?"

Joe turned back to Kane, frowning in perplexity. "Hell, Kane, I don't care if you keep him for life, but what are you talking about? Why would you need to keep him anywhere? I thought you were planning on spending some time here."

Kane grinned. "I've decided to take a job."

One of Joe's bushy eyebrows shot up.

35

"At the Four-Leaf Clover. That girl needs a foreman."

"Woman." Joe corrected him this time.

"Mmm." Kane agreed, still grinning. Then he sobered, and even Joe Devlin was reminded that the man could look as hard as the devil himself when he chose. "Don't forget, Joe, I've got my own settling up to do with the ranch."

"You're on a fool's quest, Kane."

"Maybe. But you'll keep my secret, won't you?"

"Yes, you know I will. I just thought you might want to spend some time relaxing. You know, days out at the pool sipping margaritas, catching up on some reading, riding for the pleasure of it."

"If things go my way," Kane said, slipping his hat down low over his forehead, "I will be spending a few days by the pool—but not yours, Senator!" He laughed at the puzzled expression on the older man's face. "You told me that Martine Galway was a pretty girl. You were wrong. She's the stuff dreams and fantasies are woven from."

Joe glanced at Kane with narrowing eyes. "Tread carefully with her, Kane. She's been through a lot. Don't . . ." He hesitated. Maybe he had no right to give warnings to other people, and he was more perceptive than Kane realized. Kane hadn't said much—he never did— but Joe knew that Kane had arrived at Martie's just in time to prevent some real disaster.

"Don't hurt her." He finished a little lamely. But then he chuckled, a bright light touching his eyes. "Never mind. Come to think of it, Martie Galway might be just what you need, my boy. The lady's been known to cause a heart or two to bleed."

Kane laughed again. "Sounds like you think the two of us would be fitting adversaries in some kind of arena."

"Maybe that's exactly what I mean."

Kane shrugged. "Well, you'd better excuse me, Joe, or

there will be no ranch, and I'd rather not see her face a certain other adversary again."

"By all means, get going."

Kane nodded. Joe Devlin walked him to the door. "Take the CJ-seven into town, then come back here for the horse. It will be a lot faster. Oh, and Kane, what do you want me to do if anyone asks for you?"

Kane shrugged. "No one should be asking. I'm a big kid now, Joe. I've been out on my own a long time, and I'm known to land on my feet."

"Keep in touch."

Kane nodded.

When he walked back into the sunshine, he saw the jeep parked up the drive. Senator Joseph Devlin had a tendency to be a step ahead of everyone, Kane thought with affection. He had probably ordered the jeep pulled around the second he had realized Kane had returned.

But as he left the driveway behind and headed for town, Kane wasn't thinking about Joe Devlin. He was thinking about Martine Galway, about the way he'd felt when he saw Lander pinning her to the ground.

His fingers gripped the gearshift, and he forced himself to inhale a long, shaky breath. He couldn't make trouble with Lander now—not the kind of trouble he wanted to make. Joe Devlin wanted to pin Lander with all the legal goods he could.

Besides, he thought, his scowl fading a bit as he eased back into the comfortable driver's seat of the vehicle, on one score he had something in common with Lander.

He hadn't been able to think about anything but Martine since he'd met her either. Daydreams and fantasies— just as he had told Joe. He wondered just what kind of hero he really was, saving her from the pressuring affections of one man when he would have loved to have grabbed her and swept her up a staircase himself.

He wanted her, just as Lander did. He didn't think

that any healthy male could see her and not have a few carnal thoughts.

Obsessions, he admitted. He could deny anything to her, but not to himself. He would love to have her in lieu of $8,000—in lieu of $80 for that matter. Because just like Lander, he'd envisioned her naked, decked only in that wild mane of waving hair, her eyes liquid and flashing, her flesh bared to his touch, her arms reaching for him.

Kane twisted his jaw, irritated with the tension that coiled in his body. He fumbled in his pocket for a cigarette and glanced at the rolling scenery he passed: scrub mostly; some decent grassland.

Finally he sighed, having convinced himself that there was a difference between Lander and him. He wanted her with a desire so intense that it was startling, haunting, but he wanted her to want him in return, touching him with the same longing and fascination. . . .

He grimaced. Somehow he didn't see it. She'd been grateful to him but wary too. Sparks had flown between them with the explosive quality of dry tinder.

And, he reminded himself, eyes narrowing with self-annoyance, there was something else he had to want more than a woman he had just met. There was something else more important: a promise he had made to another woman, one very, very dear to his heart.

His fool's quest, Joe called it.

What he wanted was the Four-Leaf Clover. It had to take precedence over everything.

CHAPTER TWO

Martine wasn't at all sure that she hadn't gone crazy, but by the time dusk started falling, she was out at the barbecue with a pile of the Four-Leaf Clover's best T-bone steaks. Potatoes and corn, too, were cooking in the coals, and she'd spent more than an hour cutting and washing vegetables for a colossal effort that would put most salad bars to shame.

Maybe it wasn't so crazy. If Kane Montgomery had been real and she did get to keep the ranch, it would be a celebration. And if she were going to be out by midnight, well, at least she wouldn't be leaving much food behind!

Bill Stuart was the first of her hands to come walking around the house, a quizzical frown set into his weather worn, gaunt features. She gave him a brilliant smile while he stood staring at her, holding his hat and scratching his thinning pate.

"Martie, why's the front door locked? And what's happening here? Did you get Lander to extend that loan this morning?"

The tone of his voice was suspicious and paternal. Bill and his wife, Sonia, had worked for her dad. Sonia was supposedly the cook and housekeeper, but ever since Ed Rice, the foreman, had been laid up in the hospital, Sonia had been riding cattle and fixing fences alongside her husband. Sonia didn't mind at all. She was a ball of energy, just as happy and at ease in the saddle as she was in a kitchen.

"Did you wash up, Bill?" Martine asked sweetly.

"That's not exactly the question here, is it, young woman?" Bill asked sternly, tossing his hat onto a lawn chair and picking a slice of cucumber from the bowl at the long folding table Martine had set out near the pool. "What happened this morning? And I want the truth of it! Why are you out here doing all this? Did Lander extend the loan?"

Martine dropped one of the thick steaks onto the grill. It sizzled immediately with a little cloud of smoke, and she inhaled deeply when the delicious aroma hit the air.

"Martine Galway—"

"No. Lander did not extend the loan," she replied.

"Then—"

"We're having a house barbecue anyway. I—I may have gotten a new loan."

She threw another steak on the fire, aware that Bill had planted his hands on his hips and was watching her with suspicious wariness.

"From who?"

"A man."

"Great. What man?"

Martine was saved from answering when Sonia came around the corner. She was a solid woman with ample breasts and an almost homely face that became fascinating when she smiled. She wasn't really a maternal figure at all, yet Martie had grown up with her and loved her dearly.

"Martie?" she asked instantly, her bright blue eyes probing.

Martine had to chuckle. They both were staring at her as if her own earlier suspicion were true: She must have lost her mind.

"Well, I don't know yet," she said flatly, but a smile

40

did curve her lips. "But if the world is lost, what the hell! We'll just consider it the fall of the Roman Empire and enjoy the night. Bill, go get the cooler out of the kitchen, will you? We've got lots of red wine and beer to go with rare steaks!"

"I'll get the cooler," Bill told his wife, inclining his head toward Martie. "You get Miss Effervescence over there to tell you what she's talking about!" A little put-out, Bill strode across the patio and through the back door.

Sonia walked over to Martie. "All right. What man? What's going on here?"

But once again Martie was saved from an answer because Jim Pix, her third and last hand, came around the corner, looking as confused as the Stuarts had been.

"Do I smell a barbecue? Wow, Martine, what a spread! Why's the front door locked? Did you get the loan extended? I guess you must have!" Jim was barely what Martine termed legal. He was a tall, lanky young man, just out of college, the son of a Wyoming rancher who had decided all his offspring would profit most from seeking hard work elsewhere before taking on their own ranches. He was freckled and sandy all over: light brown eyes; sun-bleached light brown hair. Jim had been certain that his dad could have—and would have—helped if only they'd had more time.

"No, I didn't get the loan extended, but I may have a new one," Martine said breezily. "Now, did everyone wash up? If not, go ahead and do so."

"Who is this man that Bill was asking you about?" Sonia demanded stoutly, adding quickly, "Yes, ma'am, we all washed up at the bunkhouse. Now—what's going on?"

Martine was once again rescued from an answer by the grand finale of all timely arrivals. She hadn't noticed him come around the house; she hadn't heard a thing. Yet even as she opened her mouth to stall again—since she had figured out no way at all to explain Kane Montgomery—she heard his voice, a low, pleasant, well-modulated drawl. "Good evening."

Martine swung about. He was in nice, worn, form-hugging jeans and a red polo shirt that enhanced his dark, rugged looks. He was hatless this evening and apparently had quite recently stepped from the shower. His jaw was clean-shaved; his hair was still damp. His eyes met hers, and he smiled slowly, expectantly.

It seemed to take her heart a few seconds to start beating again. She was relieved to see him—and a little stunned. She had desperately wanted him to come back yet the whole thing had been ludicrous. . . .

He raised a brow slightly, as if he were a little amused by her speechlessness and even her lack of manners. He stepped forward, offering an outstretched hand to Sonia. "Hi, I'm Kane Montgomery. Has Martine mentioned me yet? I'm the new foreman."

"Foreman!" Sonia exclaimed.

Everyone whirled around when Bill came out from the game room with the cooler and dropped it with surprise at Sonia's word.

Kane gazed at Martine, his head inclined to the side in query, his voice a little taunting. "I guess you haven't said anything yet, huh?"

Sonia was still staring at him, a little dazed. "Foreman?" she repeated. "Then that means we've still got a ranch!"

Martie finally recovered; the smell of charring meat did it for her. She quickly forked the meat and turned it over, drew in a deep breath, and tried to meet Kane's eyes with the same calm gaze that he was giving her.

"Bill, Sonia, Jim, this is Kane Montgomery. Mr. Montgomery, do we still have a ranch?"

He reached into his pocket, his mouth still twisted with

a small, amused grin as he walked toward her and produced a folded paper from his billfold. Her eyes glazed slightly as she stared down at the paper. She already knew what it was.

"Take it," he told her quietly.

She did. Her fingers shook a little as she unfolded it and saw her original note marked paid and notarized.

She lifted her chin slowly, looking up into his eyes. "You—you really did it," she murmured.

"Ms. Galway, did you have doubts?"

She shrugged, smiling slowly. "I have to admit that I had more than a few."

"What is going on here?" Bill demanded.

"Meat's burning—that's what's going on!" his wife declared, stepping around Martine to snatch the fork from her hand and adjust the searing meat again.

"Wait a minute!" Jim said, frowning. "We do have a ranch or we don't have a ranch?"

Martine laughed a little nervously. After all, she still owed someone $8,000. And as fascinated as she was by Kane Montgomery, she still felt a few shivers when she gazed at him, remembering quite clearly that he had shown some coercive force and real temper that morning. But so far he hadn't asked her to sign a thing. He had paid off her loan on faith.

"We have a ranch," she said to Jim, but she had not yet managed to tug her eyes from Kane's.

Bill let out a long whoop of relief and reached into the cooler for a beer. He threw it into the air and caught it. "I'll drink to that!" he proclaimed.

"Steaks are ready," Sonia announced. She moved the meat onto a platter and dug into the coals for the corn and potatoes. She paused, staring at Kane. "That is, the steaks are ready if Mr. Montgomery eats them the proper way."

43

"Black and blue!" Kane said with a laugh. "Nice and pink inside, charcoaled on the out."

"He's got to be all right," Sonia muttered. "The man knows how to eat a piece of meat." She gave Kane a big, warm smile, which, Martine knew, meant that Sonia had decided to accept him, which also meant that Bill would accept him. Jim liked everyone.

"Guess we're working for you then, Mr. Montgomery," Bill said, approaching Kane with a broad smile and a can of beer. The men shook hands; it appeared that they had sized each other up and decided in a few short seconds that they both liked what they saw.

"Martie!" Sonia prodded her. "Are we going to eat or are we going to stand around all night?"

"We're going to eat!" she said quickly.

The food was put on the table. Martine wound up between Kane and Jim, facing Sonia and Bill. She was situated evenly between the men, yet as food was passed and salt and pepper were requested and handed over, she realized that she was rivetingly aware of the man to her right, Kane.

Heat emanated from him. She sensed each contraction of his thigh, each fluid movement of his tanned arms, occasionally brushing hers like a whisper of warm air.

The steak had smelled so delicious, but now she could barely eat. She toyed with her glass of burgundy, sipping too much too quickly and growing even warmer.

She had to talk very little. Sonia and Bill were quizzing Kane in a very friendly style. And Kane was somehow answering them without really giving any answers at all. Yes, he had been in ranching all his life. No, he wasn't from around here, much farther south.

"And you happened to just walk in today when you were so badly needed. With eight thousand dollars to boot!" Sonia marveled at it with a rich chuckle.

"Well, I didn't really just happen to walk in," Kane

44

said, making Martine tense. He gazed at her with his eyes still carrying that glitter of subtle amusement, as if he were as aware of her slightest motion as she was of his. "I've, uh, worked for Senator Joe Devlin on and off over the years."

"He's back?" Martie asked, startled. She felt as if she were crashing down suddenly. It had been wonderful—a miracle, to say the least—that Kane had come along to save the ranch. But now it seemed a little too bad. If she had only known that Joe Devlin was back! Joe would have lent her the money, and then she wouldn't be in debt to a man who was—no matter how fascinating and . . . arresting he might be—still a stranger.

A stranger with a definite aura of mystery about him, not to mention an ability to be a very dangerous man.

He turned to look at her then, and she felt her body tense once again; it seemed that a shield fell over his eyes. They suddenly seemed heavy-lidded and glittered in the falling sun.

"He got back just before dawn," Kane said flatly. Then he gave his attention to Bill, asking questions about the cattle and the grazing lands and the state of the fences.

Martine took another long sip of wine. Her head seemed to be spinning. He did know cattle, and he did know horses. He had the bronzed and rugged look of a man who had really spent his life in the saddle. He appeared to be everything he was saying he was, yet somewhere deep inside her she was certain that he had to be more—much, much more.

She stood suddenly, smiling a little nervously at the gathering. "I think I'll run in and put the coffee on," she murmured. Before anyone could respond, she moved quickly over the patio and into the house.

Once she was in the parlor, she paused to lean against the wall, feeling the startling thud of her heart again.

Who was he?

45

It was the same question that had been nagging her all day, even when she had thought that he might disappear with the sunset—just as he had appeared with the dawn.

"What is the matter with me?" she whispered aloud. She should have just been grateful for what was—no matter what lay below the surface. She had her ranch. Legally. In fact, legally he was the one without a leg to stand on. Not that she wouldn't repay him his money, but he hadn't even asked her to sign a note yet. . . .

Martine pushed away from the wall and hurried into the kitchen. She quickly filled the pot with water and measured coffee into it, set it on the stove, then hurried to the phone. Her fingers, she noted, were still shaking as she dialed Joe's number.

He answered the phone himself, and she said, "Hello, Joe. This is Martie Galway."

"Martine! Young lady, I just heard about your troubles. I'm sorry I was away. I would have come by this afternoon except that by then I'd heard that it was all taken care of."

She twisted the phone wire around her finger, smiling a little bitterly at the receiver. "Actually, Joe, I did try to reach you. First, you were in a swamp of meetings. Then you left on a junket."

"But I should have gotten a message—"

Yes, you should have, Martine thought, but she didn't see any reason now to create a host of new problems for him. "I did leave my name, but when the secretary asked me if it was a matter of national emergency, I didn't think my situation qualified. Anyway, that's all past now, isn't it?" She tried to sound cheerful; she could hear him mumbling about the inefficiency of the bureaucracy. "Thanks, Joe, for caring. It seems to be okay now, but that's what I was calling you about. This man . . . Kane Montgomery, he says he knows you, that he's worked for you. Is that true?"

46

Was the senator's hesitation just a little too long? Martine wondered. Or was she just expecting it to be?

"Sure, Martie," he said at last. "I know Kane. And yes, he's, uh, worked for me."

So he was real, Martine thought. Joe Devlin had just vouched for him. What more could she want?

He still just didn't seem right.

"Martine, honey, you still there?"

"Yes, Joe, I'm sorry." She paused for just a second again. "Then he's really all right, Joe? He lent me the money I needed. How did a ranch hand happen to have eight thousand dollars—eight thousand he was immediately ready to hand over to me?"

"Well, I did know that your foreman's been hospitalized for a while now, Martie. I sent Kane over there this morning."

"Thanks." She breathed lightly. One thing she couldn't forget was the fact that Kane had really made one hell of a timely appearance that morning! "But the money—"

"Martie," Joe Devlin interrupted, "I hate to tell you this, but eight thousand dollars isn't all that much money anymore."

It was when you didn't have it, Martine thought mournfully.

"Martie," the senator said softly, "trust me. Kane is all right."

"But—"

"By the way, Martie, can you come out for dinner soon? Feels like a long time since I've seen you, young lady. And bring him."

"Bring him?"

"Yeah, Kane."

"Uh, sure, I suppose," Martie murmured. Dinner was fine, but she was still feeling ridiculously confused, and she couldn't understand why. She'd called Joe with ques-

47

tions. Well, Joe had answered her questions, assuring her that Kane Montgomery was all right.

Why did she feel Joe was hedging?

"I'll see you then, Martine."

"Uh, fine."

Joe hung up. Martine replaced the receiver slowly, and as she did it seemed as if a sizzle of fire had leaped along her spine. She spun about—and Kane was there.

His arms were crossed over his chest, and he was leaning against the wall. His eyes were narrowed, yet his lips curled in amusement. She wondered with a sudden fury just what went on in his mind, what his thoughts were beneath the devilishly sharp shields that had risen over his eyes.

"Checking up on me?" he drawled.

"Yes," she answered flatly.

He shrugged slightly, inclining his head toward her with a grimace. "And?"

"Joe Devlin seems to like you, but I'm sure you know that. And if you hadn't known it, you would have ascertained it from my side of the conversation." She hesitated for just a moment. "Didn't anyone ever tell you that eavesdropping is impolite?"

"I wasn't eavesdropping—or I didn't intend to be. I've been right here. You just didn't turn around."

"You should have made your presence known."

He shrugged again and walked across the room. "Coffee's done," he said. "What cups do you want?"

Martine hesitated, then went to the cupboard and started pulling out mugs. "Joe asked us over for dinner sometime," she said, then stopped rattling the mugs and looked at him with a dry smile. "Or did you already know that?"

"Dinner with the senator sounds good," he replied, undaunted by her tone.

"Dammit," Martie snapped, "who are you?"

He laughed with an honest humor that seemed to encompass Martine with warmth. There was something deep about that laugh. It was low and rich and . . . and pleasantly, alluringly masculine. Like his clean scent, like the quiet, confident air about him. She realized with a start that she longed to reach out and touch him, to study the angles and curves of his features with her hands and fingers, and see if she couldn't get to know him, find her answers, that way.

He was a man she barely knew, she reminded herself, a man who was still—with or without Joe's recommendation—very disturbing and mysterious.

"Martine," he said, catching her shoulders and staring down into her eyes, "I swear to you the money was mine. Saved—not begged, borrowed, or stolen. I promise you. I've worked ranches all my life. Joe Devlin vouched for me because he knows me. I don't know what else to say to you that might settle your qualms."

She felt more than a little flushed, standing that close to him, feeling his gaze and hands touch her like rays of a summer sun. She swallowed a little. No man—stranger or friend—had ever had the power to affect her so.

She tried to offer him a teasing smile. "You just rode in like the cavalry to rescue a damsel in distress. Would you have lent that money to anyone in need who could give you a job in return?"

"No," he said simply. "I lent you the money because you—" He paused as if searching for the right word, then added so softly that she felt another shiver of heat rake her spine, "you fascinate me."

"No. No strings attached," she told him breathlessly.

"No strings attached," he said in confirmation.

She drew in a deep breath and managed to pull away from his light hold on her shoulders. "There's a tray beneath the counter," she said briskly. "Sugar's on the counter; cream's in the fridge. Would you mind? I'll take the pot."

She could still feel his eyes on her. The sensation was electric, but she forced herself to ignore him, smile, and walk out of the kitchen with the coffeepot.

He followed her with the tray. "We need to discuss a little business," he said.

Martine hesitated. "Right after coffee. The house office connects to the foreman's quarters." Again she hesitated, wondering if she wasn't inviting a mountain lion straight into her home. "Inside the house," she said at last. "There's a separate entrance, a kind of whole private area. I'll show you."

She started out again, then spun around. "Except, of course, you realize that I have a permanent foreman? The job can only be temporary."

"I know the situation," Kane said flatly as he went out to the patio.

The mood at the patio table was festive. And why not? They all could have been packing, and they weren't. But as everyone else talked, Martine found herself silent again, watching her newfound rescuer/employee. He was smiling a lot, laughing. Yet she still felt something hard about him, and she sensed that the others felt it too. It was as if he might be very pleasant at the dinner table but a granite dictator when it came to work. Still, Martine didn't think her people would mind that. They were a great group, with a firm belief in a day's work for a day's pay. They all worked the ranch as hard as she did. As long as they respected Kane, she knew they wouldn't mind his authority; she suspected that anyone would wind up respecting the man.

Sonia explained to him that she and Bill had what they called the bunkhouse, except it wasn't really a bunkhouse at all; it was a beautiful little frame house that was just perfect for them. It was set about a quarter of a mile behind the barn and had a couple of rooms with a separate entrance—just like the main house—for whoever else was around.

Martine thought that Sonia should act a little worried about her being up at the main house alone with the new foreman, a stranger, but Sonia didn't appear at all concerned. Martine stared at her mug and sighed. The foreman was always in the main house, and no one had ever worried. But then Ed Rice was older than her father had been, his hair was snow white, and he was a paternal figure if Martine had ever seen one.

There was nothing remotely paternal or fraternal about Kane Montgomery. The man was pure threat—or promise, Martine wasn't sure which. Yet she was equally sure, as Sonia apparently was, that Kane would never use his strength against her—unless it was the strength of his will, which Martine decided could probably be as dangerous as the power of his lean but tautly muscled frame.

"You know, Mr. Montgomery," Jim was saying good-naturedly, "I could swear we've met before or that I've seen you somewhere."

Martine tensed, carefully watching the profile of the man beside her; it was as strong as a hawk's. He didn't sidestep the issue; he stared straight at Jim, frowned slightly, and pulled his cigarettes out of his pocket and lit one.

"No, I don't think we've met," he said at last.

Jim shrugged. "I guess not. But maybe it will come to me later."

"Well, it's getting late," Sonia said to her husband. "Let's get some of these dishes in and done and head for home."

Everyone rose and started bringing things into the main house. The effort was in unison, like all the work on the ranch, and with Sonia's competence at supervision,

51

the kitchen was soon as clean as the patio with every last dish put away.

But before Bill, Sonia, and Jim could leave, there had to be a concession to the fact that Martine still owned the ranch and that they all still had jobs. Bill hugged Martine, Sonia kissed both her cheeks enthusiastically, and even Jim got carried away enough to hug her and kiss her nose awkwardly. Finally they each shook Kane's hand again, promising to see him at dawn.

And then she was waving good night, with Kane standing behind her.

The place suddenly seemed unusually quiet. And Martine felt as if all her nerve endings had been stripped and she had become acutely aware of sensation.

She shoved her hands into her pockets, turned, and walked past Kane. "Where are your things?"

"In the barn. I'll get them later."

She nodded. "Come on down the hall, and I'll show you the office and your room."

She passed her own bedroom door, and a fit of shivers seemed to seize her. She kept walking, past the room that had been her father's and past the guest room. She took a little turn to the left, to the ell where a door stood ajar. She pushed it open and quickly, too nervously, turned on the light. There was a big oak desk in the office, silver gray filing cabinets, and the small home computer she had purchased just the year before.

"You'll find the accounts, payroll, purchases, and anything else you might want to know on disks. Neatly labeled and arranged," she said with a little laugh. "Requisitions and all are in the cabinets. But I guess we can go through all that sometime tomorrow. I've been doing the bookkeeping since Ed has been laid up." She stopped speaking and sat in the chair before the desk, indicating that Kane was welcome to the one behind it. He smiled slightly and sat, watching her.

"What happened with Ken?" she asked at last.

He shrugged. "I paid him."

"Just like that?"

"Oh, well, he wasn't really happy with the situation at first," Kane said, his voice trailing away slightly.

Martine flinched, quickly perusing his features, as if she hadn't already done so all evening. "You didn't—he didn't—"

Kane laughed. "We both were very civilized, though I admit there's something about that man that makes me long for a good fight."

"So?"

"I pointed out the legal ramifications. He was bound to take the money. I also pointed out the fact that you could bring charges against him for attempted rape and physical abuse. I don't think that had occurred to him yet."

"Oh," Martine murmured, looking down at her hands. She raised her eyes to his then. "Well, what do we do next? I'm assuming you'd like a little more than faith right now to guarantee your money."

He smiled. "Yes, I've got a note for you to sign. But tomorrow will be soon enough. Or the day after—I'm assuming that you'd like to have it checked over by your attorney."

She nodded, watching him uneasily, fascinated again by his eyes and the cast of his rugged features.

"So it really is—legitimate," she murmured.

"Completely," he told her. "I'm not the devil, and you're not signing over your soul." He stood and stared at the back door of the office. "I take it my room is back there?"

Martine nodded and rose too. He walked to the connecting door and switched on the light.

It was a massive room with a large bed covered with an old Indian spread. There was a small television, an old stereo system, an icebox, and a small Sterno burner. Ed

Rice had been with the Galways as long as the Stuarts had; he had lived in the house like family, but even family needed moments of privacy, and this back room attached to the office had been planned to afford privacy.

"Nice," he murmured, stepping into the room.

Martine followed him but paused in the doorway. "The bath leads out to the pool. On Sundays we all have a habit of sitting around a little in the afternoon and using your bath as the cabana. I hope you don't mind."

He chuckled. "It's your house." His smile flashed whitely against his bronzed cheeks. Then his long strides took him across the room, and he disappeared into the bathroom.

The door remained opened, but he didn't reappear. At last Martie frowned and followed him.

The door that led back out to the patio was open too. She stepped quickly through the bath and outside.

He was standing by the pool, looking up at the moon. He smiled when he saw her. "It's really a fabulous layout," he told her.

"Thank you," she said simply. Then she exhaled a long breath. "Uh, thank you, for everything. For this morning, for your money, for letting me keep this, for . . ." Her voice disappeared in a whisper.

He chuckled again and came to her slowly, a bit as if he were stalking her. But then he didn't really. There was nothing predatory about his movement. He just came to her. His hands rested on her shoulders, and he stared down into her eyes, his own touched by the moon and seeming to compel her to meet his stare.

"For giving you a loan with no strings attached?" he asked.

She nodded.

"No strings . . ." he murmured. There definitely was a devilish cast to his gaze now, and he lowered his head. "I would take one advantage—if you don't mind?"

"Yes?" she asked a little breathlessly.

"One kiss."

She didn't answer him. Or perhaps she did. She moistened her lips slightly with the tip of her tongue. His mouth came to hers. His hands slid evocatively down her spine to the small of her back, pressing her against his length.

She felt strength in the coercive thrust of his tongue against her lips, yet it was somehow gentle, like a rough velvet persuasion.

She slipped her hands around his neck and felt the fine cords of muscle there. Her body seemed to come alive against his, cherishing its hardness, the feel of heat and power against the softness of her breasts. He tasted slightly of beer, and his scent was that of the night, clean and musky and fascinating.

His knuckle brushed her cheek, and he slowly, savoringly lifted his lips from hers. His eyes were on hers again, and she realized that he had carefully restrained himself from any more than what he had asked. She felt tension in him, like a passion and hunger well leashed.

He smiled. "I guess I'd better let us both get some sleep, Ms. Galway. Ranch life starts early."

She nodded, still staring at him. She wasn't at all sure if she was relieved or disappointed. She felt as if her body were dancing, and she was shivering, very hot and then suddenly very cold.

She had wanted him to hold her and hold her. . . .

He was a stranger, and she had never behaved like this before in her life. But then she had never wanted a man like this before in her life. She felt as if she had been set afire, as if she couldn't care less about anything else in the world. All she wanted was to explore the heat within herself, have him touch her, lie beside him and feel his body against hers. . . .

She stepped back quickly, groping wildly in her mind

for good sense and ethics. What in God's name was wrong with her?

"Good night," she said quickly. Then she fled across the patio and returned to the house by way of the game room.

In her room she quickly donned a worn head-to-toe flannel nightgown, as if its chaste appearance could rid her body and mind of wanton fascination.

It didn't work. She lay awake half the night, painfully, achingly aware that he was in the same house.

Who was in the same house?

The great shame was that she just couldn't seem to make not knowing who he was matter that night. She couldn't make the question of his identity uppermost in her mind. He had made her burn inside, yearn and ache with desire. . . . It was an alien feeling. It was so thrilling that she could barely catch her breath, even as she lay still.

And it was frightening. Very, very frightening.

But it was undeniable. She lay awake for hours, wondering about him. She could find no answers, and she tossed about miserably.

Too late, and very close to dawn, she at last slept. But even then he haunted her dreams. He came to her in them, offering her a world of wonder and ecstasy. . . .

Then she realized that he wanted something in return, but the dream refused to tell her what.

CHAPTER THREE

No one woke Martie up in the morning. She opened her eyes in a foul humor that was made worse when she realized the sun was very high in the sky and daylight was flooding into her room.

"Damn!" she muttered, leaping out of bed to take a cool and invigorating shower. She dressed in something like a panic, then raced out of her room.

But the ranch house was empty.

In the kitchen she discovered a note: "Hope you had a nice sleep, Princess, with the castle safe once again. See you tonight. Kane."

There was coffee awaiting her on the stove. Rather than ease her sense of irritation, the coffee only increased it, not enough for her to refuse to drink a cup, but she remained irritated nevertheless. Martie hated the fact that she had overslept while everyone else was out working.

She sat down at the kitchen table to sip her coffee. "It entirely destroys my hardworking self-image!" she said aloud. And then, at last, she laughed at herself. Things were going right. Maybe she had just been under so much stress for so long that she didn't know how to handle things when they were finally going right.

She noticed by gazing around the kitchen that Kane had made himself breakfast and cleaned up after himself.

"I'll bet he even fried his bacon," she muttered, and

then once again she was laughing and trying to decide if she hated him for being perfect or just for leaving her so mentally and physically confused that she seemed incapable of normal behavior.

At that thought she was seized by tension, and all alone in the kitchen she blushed. She didn't hate him. She liked him. Actually she was fascinated by him. Maybe that was what frightened her so much. He was living in her house now and had very smoothly taken over the running of her ranch. He was attracted to her. He had said as much.

Inadvertently she put her fingers to her lips. She could still remember the feel of his lips: a touch of strength without force; a touch that was tender yet hinted of a smoldering demand; a touch that had kept her awake all night, wondering, fantasizing . . .

Martine drew in a deep breath. *Slow down,* she warned her suddenly pounding heart—and herself. Maybe the man was authentic, or maybe he was an impulsive drifter. Even so, she was over twenty-one, and she owed herself something. If he loved her and left her, wouldn't that be all right too? Surely she could feel no emotional ties—not now. Wouldn't it be okay, she mused wistfully, just to have a mad affair once in her life?

Yes, she answered herself flatly. She was a mature twenty-five-year-old woman who spent most of her life working for an inherited dream and the beloved father who had left her that dream. She deserved time for herself as well, and she was certainly of an age to decide how intimate she wanted her relations to be.

It would be okay—as long as it was honest, she decided. She didn't care about promises or guarantees, just the honesty of whatever the relationship was.

"If I only knew more about him," she murmured to herself. And she laughed out loud again because she was sitting there planning an affair with a man she had just met without being sure that an affair was what he wanted.

He hadn't asked for anything in return for the loan, she reminded herself. But then he had also more than insinuated that he did want her. . . .

Martine realized that sitting around wasn't going to do her any good. She jumped to her feet, quickly gulped down a second cup of coffee, and hurried outside to the barn. She grimaced when she saw that her buckskin, Cheyenne, was not in his stall. Someone had let him out to the pasture, and the quarter horse must have spent the morning rolling in whatever mud he could find.

In the pasture beyond the barn she found Cheyenne—every bit as filthy as she had expected. When she whistled, he trotted amiably to her, and though she started to chastise him, she quickly left off, chuckling as he nuzzled her shoulder and practically shoved her down.

"You lout!" She addressed the horse accusingly. "Now stop that and behave. You're a working horse, remember? And we're going to work today."

Martie loved the animal. He had been born on the ranch when she was a teenager. She herself had broken him in with a lot of love, and he had grown to a beautiful and sleek seventeen hands. His color was pure buff, except for his stockings, tail, and mane, and his disposition was the sweetest Martine had ever known in any horse. He had the ability to stop on a dime and race with the wind, and he was so attuned to her voice and touch that she could, if necessary, ride him bareback.

She leaned her cheek against his velvety soft nose for a moment, then patted his neck. "Get over here, boy. You are a mess!"

Ten minutes of grooming shed him of his dust and mud. He lowered his head to accept his bit. Then she led him through the barn to the tack room because his saddle was heavy and she didn't want to walk with it any farther than she had to.

Moments later she was trotting past the front pasture where the mares were running with their foals.

"Where do you think they'll be, Cheyenne?" she asked. His long ears pricked up, and she patted his rump. "By the stream? Sounds logical. Or how about the eastern sector, where the fences were down? Eastern sector, huh? Okay, we'll try that first."

Martine gave the buckskin a free rein after they had curved around the pasture. The land here was flat with only a little scrub, and she could let him race his heart out with no worry about rocks or boulders against his hooves. And he wanted to run today, just as she did. His muscles bunched beneath her with tremendous power, and the air swept by her like a cool, sweet tempest.

She leaned low to his neck and for a moment closed her eyes to feel the thunderous beat. She had almost lost everything. And suddenly she felt exhilarated and wonderful, knowing that she hadn't.

Near the hills she pulled in on their gait and began to scan the fences. At last she saw Kane. The bay he had ridden yesterday was roaming free, tugging at the patches of grass he could find. Kane had his shirtsleeves rolled up and was hammering in a fallen post. Martine wasn't sure he saw her at first; she walked Cheyenne slowly to him, drawn by the play of his muscles, naked and flexed on his forearm, straining the fabric of his shirt at his shoulders. His hat was near him on the ground, and a thatch of his dark hair had fallen over his forehead. As she at last came before him, he shoved back his hair and wiped his forehead with the back of his hand, then raised his hand in greeting since he was holding several nails in his mouth.

"Want some help?" she asked, dismounting from

Cheyenne. The amiable buckskin ambled off to search for scrub along with the bay.

He lowered his head to spit the nails into his hand, then gazed at her again. "I think I can handle a post," he said dryly. But a smile seemed to hover on his lips, as if he were glad she had come.

"Where are the others?" Martine asked.

"Rounding the cattle to the stream," he replied. His gaze moved over her, taking in her wild, windswept hair, the way her worn and faded jeans hugged her hips, the way her shirt molded over her breasts.

But it wasn't a lascivious gaze, Martie thought, wondering why she wasn't offended. It wasn't lascivious, but it was very, very sexual. She wondered again just exactly what was wrong with her. His eyes upon her made her feel warm, as if heated nectar roamed through her veins.

"Got a minute?" he asked, inclining his head toward the post. "Let me finish this up, and then I've got a few questions."

Martine shrugged. "I'm all yours," she murmured. At his smile she realized what she had said, groaned inwardly, and wandered over to the horses. She heard the thud of the hammer and turned around, fascinated again by the simple physical action. A few moments later he had hammered in the last nail. He stooped for his hat and a piece of the broken fencing, then came over to her.

"What's the matter?" she asked, frowning.

"Take a look at the wood," he told her.

She did so and saw nothing but the broken split. She looked into his eyes, mystified. "It's broken," she told him. "That's why it needed to be fixed."

"I know it's broken!" he exclaimed impatiently. "But look at the way it's split—as if someone had deliberately pulled it out."

"Or," Martine commented, determined not to be

61

cowed by the man she had hired as foreman, "as if it had been shoved out. One of the steers might have done it."

He tossed the wood down with disgust and planted his hands on his hips. "How many times have you seen a domestic steer butt a fence post like that?"

She shrugged. "It could have happened."

He threw his hands up in the air. "Okay, it could have happened. But I'm saying it didn't. And you're short one hell of a lot of cattle to call this place a ranch!"

Martie backed up slightly, then rigidly stood her ground, hooking her thumbs into her pockets. "We've had some problems. That's why I couldn't pay the loan. We lost half the herd to hoof-and-mouth, and the government ordered some of them killed before it could spread around."

"A viral disease that *didn't* spread around, did it?"

"No . . ." Martine said slowly. "But why would it have spread around from here? We were quarantined; I followed all the government instructions to the letter." She shook her head. "What are you saying?"

He shrugged. "Hoof-and-mouth on only *your* ranch, but no contaminated feed in the area. A virus can be injected. I think Mr. Lander had a hand in all this. There were too many fences down on this place, too many strange coincidences. For one, that loss of cattle was ridiculous, it should never have happened to just your herd. He didn't want you to be able to repay that loan."

Martine paused, feeling as if a little of her breath had been stolen away. It was possible. "Okay. Maybe what you're saying is possible, but how do I prove it?"

"You don't—now," Kane said a little bitterly. He planted his hands on his hips and stared up at the sun, centered in the sky. Then his eyes became riveted to hers again. "That leaves me curious all over again. Either you really did do something to that man or he was exceptionally keen to get his hands on this particular property. Which was it, Martine?"

She stared at him for a long, speechless moment, feeling her temper soar. When she spoke, her words were like chips of ice. "You might have lent me some money, Mr. Montgomery, but I'll be damned if I'll stand here on my own property and listen to any kind of veiled accusations from you!"

She spun about on her heel but was so angry that she had to grope blindly for Cheyenne's trailing reins.

His fingers were suddenly winding around her arm, pulling her back to meet him. She stared at him furiously; his features remained as intense, his eyes as probing.

"I'm sorry, Martine. I just have to know."

"You're sorry, and you're still interrogating me?" she demanded hotly.

"Yes," he said. She saw that the shields were over his eyes again; they were narrowed and piercing enigmas.

"What difference does it make?" she asked as she tugged her arm. "You've saved the day. The hero rode in, and all is well. I owe you the money now with no strings attached, remember?"

He released her and crossed his arms over his chest. "All right, Martine, have it your way. The papers are on the desk if you want to look them over and have them checked by your attorney. Why don't you go do that now?"

"I will," she said coolly, and for the first time in her life, she had trouble setting her foot in the stirrup to straddle Cheyenne's back.

His hands clamped around her waist despite her gasp of protest, and she found herself seated, staring down at him.

"And while you're at the desk, you'd better check around for cattle prices. You've got to increase this herd or it will be worthless."

63

"Don't be ridiculous," she told him. "I can't go out purchasing cattle right now. My account is cleaned out. You should know that," she snapped dryly.

But he wasn't looking at her anymore. He was gazing at the distant hills, and it seemed he was oblivious of the fact that he had angered her.

Perhaps he was aware, she thought resentfully, but figured it just didn't matter.

His eyes met hers again. "Never mind. Leave it to me. I'll do the purchasing."

"With what?"

He appeared mildly amused. "I'll rob a train," he told her, and at her thunderous expression and the spark in her eyes he laughed. "Seriously, I'll buy the cattle with my own funds."

"What are you—a bank?" She flared up at him, glad that at least when she was seated on Cheyenne, she could look down on him. "I'm not sure I want to borrow any more money from you."

He arched a dark brow in surprise. "Why? There are no strings attached."

"Aren't there?" she demanded. "It seems you've already forgotten that I own the ranch. You're the foreman, the employee."

"You hired me to do a job," he told her, and she saw the firm set to his jaw. "I'm doing it my own way."

"Ah. And would you lend me more money if I asked you to leave the ranch?" Martine asked caustically.

"No," he said flatly. "I'm not that generous."

"We'll discuss it later," she said coolly. She backed Cheyenne away from him, then turned the buckskin smoothly and nudged him into a gallop.

At that particular moment she couldn't get away from Kane Montgomery fast enough.

* * *

She read the promissory note Kane had written up in the office. It looked good—too good. His interest rate was only eight percent, and she had more than four years to make the loan good.

Tapping her foot with irritation, she saw that his signature had been notarized. Joe Devlin had vouched for him, so what was her problem?

She didn't know, but as she continued to tap her foot she decided she'd pay Joe a surprise visit—without Kane Montgomery.

Martine decided to drive the distance rather than ride, so even in her ancient Ford truck she was at Joe's door in thirty minutes. Serita, Joe's housekeeper, led her into the foyer, giving her a firm tongue-lashing for staying away so long.

"When the senator is away, it is no reason for you to be a stranger here!" Serita said chidingly. She was a slim woman with huge dark eyes and a very, very maternal attitude.

"I've had a few problems lately," Martie told her dryly.

"And you did not come to tell me all about them?" Serita demanded angrily. Martine lowered her head to hide a chuckle. She had solved problems many times in Serita's kitchen: She'd cried there when her first pony died; she'd gone there when she'd had her heart broken for the very first time in seventh grade; Joe's son, Bart, had been one of her best friends growing up. This place, this ranch, these people—all meant a great deal to her.

"Serita, I promise I'll come cry on your shoulder more often in the future," she said solemnly.

Serita gave her an indignant sniff. "Come out to the pool. The senator is relaxing. You want a margarita?"

"Sounds good. Thanks."

Joe was on one of the lounge chairs by the pool. He

65

seemed startled by Martine's appearance and looked behind her as if he hadn't expected her to be alone.

Martine bent down and kissed his cheek. "Hi, Joe. I've missed you."

He gave her a nice hug. "I'm sorry I wasn't here when you needed me."

She shrugged. "Well, it seems to be working out now."

"But to sign such a ridiculous note over to Lander, Martine. You should have known it would only cause trouble, honey."

Martie sat on one of the lounges next to him and thanked Serita when she was handed a margarita. Serita sat down with a pile of mending. "I never did think your daddy to raise no fool, child, but that was sheer stupidity!" Serita said, giving her opinion.

Martine laughed dryly. "My Lord, this sounds like *Peyton Place!* Does everyone know what I did?"

"Probably," Joe told her good-naturedly.

"You sent Kane Montgomery over because you knew exactly what was happening, didn't you?" she asked accusingly.

White lashes fell over the senator's striking blue eyes. "Maybe I did. I didn't know if you'd get yourself out of it or not. Don't begrudge me—"

"Who is he, Joe?"

He gazed at her, startled. Martine thought that Serita's sewing needle suddenly went very still.

"He's a . . . ranch foreman," Joe said.

"You're lying to me. Why?"

"Young lady," the senator said huffily, "I'm not lying to you. That man is a rancher. Anybody who's not blind can see that for a fact."

"Now he wants to lend me more money for cattle," Martine said.

Serita muttered something in Spanish.

"What?" Martine asked, only to be told she was a

stubborn and independent little whelp. Joe started laughing.

"I think she's trying to tell you to let the man give you a hand, Martie. God knows, ranching is hard enough. But throw in a few flukes like the problems you've had lately, and a saint himself could use a little assistance! I agree with her. He's a good man. Let him buy you a few cows. I guarantee that he can make you more than enough to pay him back."

Martine sighed and sipped her drink. It was good, and it was relaxing. She crossed her feet up on the lounge and leaned back. "Joe, I don't know what's going on here, but if you say I haven't anything to lose, I'll accept it."

"Good," Joe said simply.

"How's the clean air bill going?" she asked.

He gave her a rundown on the session he had just attended, then asked after Sonia, Bill, and Jim and told her he had just been to the hospital to see Ed Rice.

"Oh, God!" she groaned. "I have to get back in to see Ed. I haven't been there in a week."

"I'm sure he understands," Joe said.

Martine stayed a little longer while Joe told her how Bart was doing with his legal practice in Tucson.

She decided then that she'd better get going since she was the cook these days for four hungry workers.

"Joe . . ." she said at the door.

"Martine, would I hurt you?" he asked quietly.

"Not purposely, no," she told him. Then she sighed, gave him a kiss good-bye.

"How about that dinner a week from this Friday? Dress up, too, honey, we'll make a night of it."

"Sure," she replied.

Back at the ranch she mixed up a huge pot of stew. At eight o'clock the hands started returning. Jim and Bill were in good moods since every last fence on the place

67

was solid again, the stream was high, and the weather people were forecasting more rain.

"Things are looking up, yes, sirree!" Bill said, pinching Martine's cheek. "That man you found, lady, is one hell of a rancher!"

"That man" had obviously been in the shower. Martine jumped slightly when he suddenly appeared in the kitchen, his still-damp hair slicked back, his jeans as worn as the ones he had been wearing earlier but very clean, his shirt tonight a white cotton with rolled-up sleeves that emphasized the delineations in the muscles of his bronzed arms.

"Pot's on the stove," she told them all cheerfully. "If everyone's in, I'll run out and feed the horses."

"They've already been fed," Kane said, moving into the kitchen. He barely glanced her way.

Jim told him that he was pretty sure they had a puma down from the mountains since they were missing a few calves. "Want me to take a look around the cliffs tomorrow?"

Kane had reached into the refrigerator for a beer. He drank a long sip, then shook his head. "No, I'll go out first thing. I hate like hell to have to kill the damn things, but when they come down after the calves . . ."

When his voice trailed away, Martie gnawed lightly at her lower lip while she stirred the stew in the pot. There was a real regret in his voice when he talked about stalking down the wildcat. It was much the same way she felt; she knew that mountain lions were growing few and far between, yet what else could be done when they were killing cattle?

"Maybe we could trap it," she murmured.

"What?" Kane asked.

She realized she had interrupted a new conversation, that they had moved on to the need to buy more hay tomorrow.

"The cat. Maybe we could trap it instead of trying to kill it."

Kane shrugged. "We can try. I'll set some traps tomorrow."

She nodded, then said, "Well, this is it, soup's on. We're in the dining room tonight."

Conversation was subdued; it seemed that everyone was tired. Kane excused himself early, and Martie heard the door to the office close. Right after coffee and dessert the others filed out. They all looked tired but happy.

Sonia gave her a big kiss before leaving again. "Honey, I think we're really going to make it this time!"

Martie smiled. When they were gone, she cleaned up the kitchen and pulled bacon out of the freezer for the morning. A few moments later she heard hoofbeats outside. Frowning, she hurried into the living room and looked out the bay window.

Kane was riding away on the big bay called Thor.

She stared out the window for a while, annoyed that she was wondering where he was going. It was none of her business.

Or was it? There still seemed to be some secret about him, and she wasn't sure just how it involved her, only that it did.

Determined to get a decent night's sleep, she went to bed. But she didn't fall asleep, she just tossed and turned until she heard the hoofbeats again at midnight, and she knew Kane had returned.

By the time he appeared in the kitchen in the morning, she had a huge breakfast of pancakes, eggs, and bacon ready. He came in and helped himself at the coffeepot with a brief "good morning," then stared at the single plate on the table.

"You're not eating?"

"I already did," she said, lying. Smiling sweetly, she

69

handed him his plate and pulled her shoulder bag off the peg by the door. "I'm going to Holliman's for the hay. See you later," she said cheerfully, then left.

She made a point of spending the day out. While Ted Holliman's sons loaded her truck with hay, she took a walk with Ted to admire his yearling Arabian foal. She had coffee with his wife, then drove into town to visit a notary with the note Kane had typed out—in triplicate, she discovered when she and the young woman at the bank went through the papers. Martine had been expecting the young woman to say something about Kane, but she didn't. Apparently his funds weren't coming from anywhere in town.

She went grocery shopping next, determined to thrill them all with her prowess at an Italian meal. She bought the ingredients for chicken marsala and linguine with clam sauce, and she even decided to splurge on oysters Rockefeller.

But when everyone else came into the kitchen that night, Kane was not with them.

Martie listened to Jim's enthusiastic oohs and aahs and Sonia's assertion that meals had never looked so good. She smiled vaguely, thanked them both, and asked, "What happened to our foreman?"

"Kane?" Bill said, helping himself to a soda. "He said something about having dinner plans tonight."

"Now that's not what he said at all!" Sonia affectionately chastised her husband. "He said to apologize to Martie for such late notice, but that he had some business to take care of at dinnertime!"

"Thanks, Sonia," Martine said, trying to keep smiling. Her whole dinner and all the effort seemed such a waste. It was a horrible attitude, she knew, because the others really did enjoy everything. Jim said it was the best meal he'd ever had.

"I swear, Martie, I don't remember your being this fine a cook before!" Bill proclaimed.

They all stayed around late that night, chatting over the Italian ices she had bought. Martie tried to keep up with the conversation, but she just felt lethargic.

"I'll do the dishes, Martie," Sonia told her. That woke her up.

"Don't be crazy, Sonia, you've been out working all day!"

"Martie, I'll tell you, in all these years of doing a bit of everything, I've learned that raising kids and keeping house is the hardest job in the world."

"I haven't got any kids." Martie reminded her with a smile.

"Yes, but you went out and bought the hay and did the shopping and the cooking, the setting up, and all the cleaning that went with it. You—" She broke off at Martie's look of dismay. "What's the matter."

"The hay! I forgot to unload the hay. Oh, damn! And it's so late now."

"Hay's in," Bill said calmly, lighting up his old pipe and easing back in his chair. "Kane saw it when we came and said he'd take care of it since he wasn't staying for dinner."

"Oh," she murmured, trying to give Bill a smile. It came off weakly, she was certain. Damn Kane! Didn't he ever mess up?

Yes! He had messed up her beautiful plan to prove what a cool and collected and efficient woman she could be!

Oh, hell, why did she have to prove anything to him? she wondered bleakly.

"Sonia," she said as she rose, "I've got an idea. Let's do these together, and then we'll finish up the evening with a mulled brandy. What do you say?"

Her brandy was another success—maybe too much of

71

one. By the time they all trooped out she was feeling extremely mellow.

Martine took a long bubble bath, sipping a second brandy in the tub. When she finished, she thought she would sleep as peacefully as an infant.

But she just wasn't tired. She donned her one elegant robe—a forest green velvet with a lighter colored silk sash and lining—and wandered into the game room. Hot tears stung her eyes for a moment as she gazed at the pool table. Her father had loved the game.

She set down her brandy and set up the balls. "This one's for you, Dad," she murmured nostalgically, and tried to set a sober eye at the balls. A little cry of delight escaped her at her break. It was almost perfect. Then she heard the sound of applause.

Looking up, she saw Kane standing by the door.

"Good evening, Ms. Galway," he said, grinning. She stared at him blanky, her stick in her hand, her torso leaning halfway over the table.

Wherever he had gone, she thought, he had dressed up to go there. She had never seem him in a suit before. The slacks were tan, the jacket was a shade darker, and his vest was a chocolate brown. The combination was superb against his dark coloring. He seemed very tall and, suddenly, exceptionally good-looking. Still not really handsome but striking and rugged and, yes, almost elegant. He appeared as comfortable in the suit as he had in jeans, just different.

When his grin widened, she noted the cleft in his chin and that his dimples—the softening point of his rather severe features—were very deep.

"Sorry," he said. "I didn't mean to startle you. Want an opponent?"

She straightened, shrugging. "Do you play?"

"Don't all hustlers and drifters play pool?" He re-

72

moved his jacket and neatly folded it over the back of a chair.

She didn't move as he came around by her to pluck a pool cue from the wall. She smiled slightly. "Are you a drifter or a hustler?"

He indicated the table. "Take your shot, Ms. Galway. I believe you knocked in the six ball with your break."

She scanned the table, chose a shot, and called it. The ball sailed like magic into the chosen pocket.

"Very good." He commended her lightly. She cast him a dry glance, then called her next shot. She noted him picking up her brandy glass, swirling the liquid around, sniffing it, tasting it.

She missed her shot.

"Your fault," she told him, plucking her glass from his hand. "Go get your own brandy."

He laughed. "So that's what you've been into tonight. Brandy, huh? Why don't you play hostess and get me one?"

"Maybe I will," she replied sweetly. "But take your shot first."

"Don't trust me, huh?"

She swirled her brandy, smiling complacently. "Not for a second," she told him flatly.

He grimaced, then appeared very businesslike suddenly as he called his shot.

That ball did exactly as he ordered. And the next, and the next, and the next—until he had taken the game.

Martie kept smiling. "Are you always this good?"

"Nope," he said, returning his cue to the wall. He grinned at her and arched a brow slightly. "Tonight just seems to be my night. Do I get that brandy?"

Martine shrugged, then turned to sail gracefully out of the game room. But her attempt at gracefulness was wasted when she tripped over the small step up to the living room.

73

His light chuckle sounded behind her. "I don't think *you* should have another."

She righted herself, keeping her sweet smile plastered to her face. "Why not?" she asked lightly. "I'm not driving. All I have to do tonight is go to sleep."

The warm, enveloping sound of his laughter followed her to the kitchen. The brandy was still warming in the fondue pot. Feeling as if she were floating in a pleasant, exciting, and slightly dangerous dream, Martie sprinkled a little more cinnamon into the warming liquid, then poured out a snifter for Kane.

She thought about his words of warning, shrugged, and prepared another for herself.

When she returned to the game room—walking very, very carefully—she discovered that he had shed his tie and vest and was studying the TV page of the newspaper.

"There's a great old horror flick on," he told her. "Peter Cushing and Christopher Lee in *The Mummy*. Want to watch it?"

She waved a hand airily, almost spilling the contents of a snifter, but Kane rescued it from her hand. "Turn on whatever you like," she told him grandly. Then she noticed the speculative humor in his eyes and realized that her words, once again, could be taken in several ways. She decided to ignore the fact that she had said them.

Kane walked over to the television, flicked it on, and played with the dials for several seconds. Martine watched him, sipping her brandy.

He looked past her to the old plump leather-upholstered divan that faced the television. He lifted a hand toward it. "Want to sit with me?"

"Why not?" Martine murmured.

He walked over, caught her free hand, and led her to the sofa. Curling her toes beneath her, she sat beside him. She could feel her hand still resting in his, while she continued to sip the brandy that was going down all too easily and all too quickly. Peter Cushing was telling an inspector all about his father's find in Egypt and trying to convince the doubting policeman that a mummy really did exist.

"Want to hand me your glass?" Kane asked her. "It's empty."

"Oh. Sure." She handed him the glass and stared at the screen. "Christopher Lee makes a great mummy," she murmured.

"Mmm. I love these old things," Kane said.

"Do you really?" She chanced a glance at him. He wasn't watching the TV at all. He was staring at her, just short of laughing out loud at her.

"Do you do this often?" he asked.

"What?" she demanded a little sharply, at which point he did laugh.

"Get tipsy all by yourself."

"All by myself? I wasn't all by myself. The rest of my employees made it for dinner."

He tossed back his head slightly, and deep laughter rumbled from him, seeming to touch her insides. "So that's another mark against me. I didn't show for dinner."

"Mr. Montgomery—"

"Whoa, what a mark against me! All of a sudden I'm 'Mr. Montgomery' again!"

"Mr. Montgomery," she continued, pronouncing each of her words with careful deliberation, "it is none of my concern if you choose to eat or not."

"Oh, no?"

"Certainly not!"

He grinned and changed the direction of the conversation. "Ms. Galway, you are sloshed. Only slightly perhaps, but definitely on the way to very. Want to put your head on my lap and watch mummies until you pass out?"

"I never pass out!" she protested. "And I'm not sloshed. Not even a little."

He stretched an arm out, cupped her nape with his hand, and pulled her down. To her amazement she didn't fight him. Nor did she gaze at the screen. She stared into his eyes, wondering why it felt so right to be there.

"Okay, we'll go back to tipsy," he said. His smile seemed very gentle, almost tender, and he brought his palm to her cheek, which he caressed lightly. "You were jealous, weren't you?" he said teasingly.

"Certainly not," she replied, but her voice came out a little breathless. The rough-tender movement of his hand over the soft flesh of her face was as hypnotic as his eyes were. Not really aware of what she was doing, she reached up to brush that stray lock of dark hair back against his forehead.

"It doesn't matter at all to you where I went?" he asked in a whisper that seemed to rasp against her heart and send it into an erratic gallop.

"Of course not," she said, smiling sweetly and giving in to the temptation to explore the high bones of his cheeks with her fingers.

He caught her fingers and kissed their tips, then held them to his mouth, teasing them with his tongue. Martine felt something deep in her abdomen seem to melt like liquid fire.

"You really don't want to know where I went?" he taunted her with a smile.

"No," she said flatly. Then: "Where did you go?"

He chuckled. "A business appointment. I promise. Nothing that wasn't important would take me away from you."

"Really?" She tried to sound totally indifferent.

"Mmm . . ." he murmured, still playing with her fingers, running his teeth lightly over the pad of her pinkie. She inhaled sharply and exhaled very slowly, still staring into his eyes, so beguiled that she could not tear away. Then he entwined his fingers with hers; his large hand, very tan and strong, seemed to engulf her own. He brought their folded hands over her lap and smiled at her tenderly.

"Why do you fascinate me so?" she asked, suddenly feeling just a bit wary but also feeling the warming, lulling effects of the brandy and a strange sensation that being here, on his lap, was right and exciting and wonderfully comfortable.

"I don't know," he answered seriously, "but I'm awfully glad I do."

Her lips curled into a wistful, beautiful smile. "Why?"

Kane had been enjoying the evening immensely, but playing it with great restraint. That was difficult—close to impossible—when he was holding her, when her hair was lying like velvet over his legs and all her feminine curves were within his reach. He was holding her, feeling all her warmth, the vibrance that was so much a part of her beauty. Her flesh—he could almost feel it beneath the velvet of her robe. He caressed the curve of her hip, and the V of her robe gave a hint of the firm fullness of her breasts. He longed with all his heart to take full advantage of the moment, but he didn't want it to be this way.

"Because you fascinate me," he told her honestly. Her eyes were so large, he thought, trusting and curious—and still wary.

He caressed her cheek lightly and smoothed her tangled hair from her face. "I'm taking you to bed," he told her.

Her eyes grew even wider, and he laughed as he slipped his arms beneath her shoulder and knees to rise.

Her arms locked around his neck, but the stunned alarm was still in her eyes.

"I'm taking you to your bed, where I'm going to leave you alone," he told her, grinning. "The first time we make love, you might precede the act with, say, one glass of wine. But you won't be the least bit tipsy. You'll be wide-awake and very much aware of each sensation, and you'll be filled with passionate energy."

"Oh, really?"

"Really." His voice was low, deep—and totally confident.

CHAPTER FOUR

They all let her oversleep again. It was eleven when she jumped out of the bed with her head pounding, and of course, everyone was already gone.

An aspirin and two cups of coffee made her feel a little like living again. So did the vow she made to her stomach that she would never even sniff brandy again.

Martine spent the day industriously cleaning out stalls and the tack room. She worked with a vicious will, determined that she might as well make the tempest in her mind a useful one to get things done. She didn't leave a saddle or bridle unoiled, nor when she had finished with that task, did she leave one of the horses in peace. They were all curried and groomed to perfection.

She remembered the night before exactly—every word spoken, every nuance of movement. She thought that she should be a little ashamed by her behavior, but she wasn't. She kept telling herself that she barely knew the man and that she would have willingly fallen into bed with him in an instant. She didn't really trust him, so she had to be a little insane!

But throughout the day she just kept coming up with one conclusion: She did want him, whether it was right or wrong—or crazy. And he wanted her. It seemed to be only a matter of time.

Combing out Cheyenne's long mane, she decided that she needed time between them. She wasn't going to be embarrassed or awkward when she saw him again, but she was going to be the one to pull in the reins. Going to the senator's for dinner could be a little like a first date. Maybe she could ask him where he came from, when his birthday was, how many siblings he had, and a million other things she could think of.

"Hey, there."

She froze a little, inwardly bemoaning the fact that she had spent the day shoveling out the stalls. She was sweaty and filthy and certainly much less than fragrant, and Kane was standing at the barn door to assure her that she didn't need to speak of the devil but merely to think of him for him to make an appearance.

"Hi," she murmured back, looking around Cheyenne's long neck.

He walked up to her and sat on one of the corded stacks of hay, idly drawing out a strand to chew as he regarded her, his eyes heavy-lidded with some secret amusement.

His gaze took in the place, the neatly raked dirt, the clean stalls, the gleaming leather trappings on the tack room shelves.

"Been busy, I see."

She shrugged. "Things need to be done."

"That they do," he said pleasantly, leaning on his elbows. He smiled. "I'd thought you might be nursing a headache."

She arched a brow and smiled at him sweetly. "Not at all," she said innocently, lying, of course. She allowed her gaze to meet his and inquired lightly, "What is this? The new foreman's goofing off on the job already? Really, Mr. Montgomery, I expected much more from you."

He cast back his head and laughed easily, then patted the hay next to him. "Even the lowest employee gets a break here and there, Ms. Galway. Bosses should take breaks too. Come and sit."

80

She shook her head, saying dryly, "I smell like a stall."

"I'm sitting next to the stall. My nose will never know the difference."

"Ah, but you see, I would," she told him.

He got to his feet, slowly walked to her, clutched her hands, and forced her to turn around and look at him. His eyes were bright with amusement and a touch of fever, and he lowered his mouth to hers slowly. He kissed her lightly, murmuring his appreciation, and then kissed her again more deeply, slowly, and fully as if he were exploring her mouth and finding it infinitely sweet. His touch was beguiling, and she found herself leaning against him, a little awed by the way her blood warmed at his kiss.

But he didn't force any more. He broke away from her, still holding her hands. "Will you leave that poor gelding alone?" he said teasingly. "He's a male. Males do not like to be primped."

"Oh, they don't?" Martie murmured, watching him with wide eyes, her breath coming a little erratically.

"No."

"They don't like attention?"

"Oh, they love attention."

"That's interesting."

"I'm glad you think so," he murmured, flashing her a white smile. Staring at his mouth, she remembered the erotic way his teeth had moved over her fingertips the night before, and it occurred to her that he was probably a very experienced lover and that he was probably equally accustomed to having his way.

"Come on over and sit with me a minute. I want to talk to you."

She shrugged and allowed him to lead her to the hay bale, curious about his next move.

But it wasn't moves he had in mind. Not the type she had been thinking of at any rate.

"Martine, I want to bring in more cattle. I talked to Holliman on the phone just now, and he gave me a great lead on some young Brahmans. What do you say?"

She stiffened. "That puts me a lot further into debt, doesn't it?"

He spit out an impatient oath, releasing her hands to stand and pace the dirt floor in front of her. "Lady, you took one hell of a chance when you signed that note to Ken Lander. What is your problem with doing something legitimate?"

She hesitated, staring down at her hands.

"Martine, I'm trying to help you make a go of this place!" he said, coming before her earnestly to get down on one knee and grip her hands again, heedless of the dirt. He smiled suddenly and pulled a handkerchief from his back pocket to wipe a speck of dirt off her nose. "Admit it. I gave you one of the best loans in history! If you fired me tomorrow, the terms wouldn't change. Tell me, just what is your problem with this?"

"I don't know," she muttered. Then she smiled at him a little ruefully, a little cynically. "No strings attached?"

"No strings attached."

"If I fired you tomorrow, you'd leave?"

He hesitated. "Would you do that?"

"I could. You never know," she murmured, seeking his reaction. Surprisingly she did get one from him. He stood up and absently rubbed his chin as he wandered over to Cheyenne and then back.

"Okay," he said a little harshly. "You seem to want terms. You seem to think that something has to have a catch for it to be real."

She leaned back in the hay, bracing herself mentally and physically. "I just can't figure this out, Kane," she said bluntly. "You don't look or act a thing like Mary Poppins or the Rainmaker. So what is this? You walked in—rode in, actually—out of the blue, right in the nick of time. My ranch is saved from the dastardly villain."

"More than your ranch was saved." He reminded her sharply.

"I never questioned that," she said smoothly. "Nor have I shown a lack of gratitude. I just don't understand what's going on. I thought you were a drifter. Few drifters drift around with your kind of money. And with your kind of money you don't seriously need a job. So what are you really after?"

Outside, a cloud must have passed over the sun. The barn was suddenly cast into shadow when she most needed clarity.

She could see nothing but his tall form, hands on his hips, feet firm on the ground, his profile rugged and harsh.

"You," he told her flatly.

She started to laugh. "But you'd never even seen me before the day you came here!"

"That's true," he said, and even with the shadows suddenly filling the barn, she was clearly aware that he was stalking toward her. She thought to back away too late; he caught her shoulders, and she was suddenly lying in the hay with him above her, not hurting her but trapping her between the span of his arms.

"Kane—"

"I came here that day," he interrupted with raw determination, "because Joe Devlin suggested it. We both know that. But I didn't offer you the loan until I'd seen you. And I didn't offer another loan for the cattle until I'd seen the ranch—and more of you. Now, Ms. Galway, we both know that there's something going on between us. Call it chemistry, call it whatever you like. It—"

"It might well be a figment of your imagination!" Martie exclaimed, angry and suddenly more than a little frightened. Not that he would hurt her, but he was very right, and he could prove it—and she would still be as lost as she was now.

"I don't think so," he told her, his eyes narrowing still further in the dim light. "Not after last night—not before last night really. Now I'm not sure what your problem is, not with the loan but with me. You're like fire and ice. If you want to be honest, you'll admit that last night could have been mine completely. That's not the way I want it. Not for us, because I'll never give you a chance to have any excuse to deny anything after the fact. Maybe you've got a hang-up about knowing someone well. Or maybe you want the dinner and flowers routine first. Well, I'm not a game player, Martine. Maybe you are. Maybe you feel you have to have some kind of excuse to go to bed with a man other than the fact that you just want to. Want me to make it easy for you? Want me to make it part of a demand?"

"You wouldn't," she replied on a breath of fury and shock.

"You're right," he said flatly. "I wouldn't." He smiled suddenly. "Especially since it wouldn't matter in the least. My feelings are too intense for deals or games—and I think yours are too. It's going to be a short matter of time before you're mine, Ms. Galway, and the ranch, the money, the loans—nothing will have a damned thing to do with it!"

"Why, you—you," Martie sputtered, "you cocky, arrogant, SOB!"

He shook his head a little ruefully and suddenly moved away from her, freeing her from the prison of his arms. "Not guilty!" he told her lightly, and his smile flashed against his bronzed features again. "Determined and confident maybe. And"—his voice fell to an intense whisper that riddled her spine with a surging fever—"insatiably hungry . . ."

He turned and headed for the door. "I'm taking the

truck. I'm off to buy the cattle. I won't be back until late probably. I'm sure I can do something else with them if we can't come to an agreement."

Martine fumbled to sit up in the hay, trying to fight the spell of his words and take control. But he was still claiming there were no strings attached; he wasn't asking her for anything, and she'd be a fool to turn down terms as good as his.

What was her problem?

He paused at the door, turning back. "You want a catch, Ms. Galway? All right. I want this job for at least a month. There's no way Ed Rice can pick it up before then."

He stayed there, waiting, still caught in shadow so that she read no emotion on his features.

She stood up, planting her thumbs in her pockets and stiffening her spine. "That's your catch? Why?"

"Why? Catches don't get explained, Ms. Galway. That's why you get to call them catches or strings that are attached."

She hesitated, watching him.

"Well? Do you want some cattle? Do you want to give your ranch a fighting chance?"

"Oh, damn the cattle!" she told him irritably.

He smiled. The shadows couldn't hide the triumphant gleam in his eyes or that white flash of his teeth.

Why shouldn't he smile? He'd gotten his way.

"There's something else you should know, Ms. Galway," he added mockingly.

"And what's that?" She lifted her chin.

"When I say mine, I mean mine. My intentions are passionate and carnal—and quite honorable. I intend to marry you too."

She frowned instantly, but to no avail. He was already gone, and she was suddenly shaking too badly to go racing after him.

* * *

That night Martie discovered she was too restless to do anything. She'd cleaned the kitchen spotlessly after dinner, vacuumed the entire house, dusted, and done two loads of laundry.

She'd even decided that Kane Montgomery was definitely good for one thing: making her productive simply because he made her so unsettled that she had to find an outlet for her energy.

At eleven o'clock he still wasn't back. She made herself a cup of tea and eventually wandered outside with it. The clouds that had brought shadows that afternoon had also brought a little rain, but the sky was clear again. Everything seemed fresh, and the air carried a beautiful scent of flowers on it.

Martine watched the play of the moon and the house lights on the water of the pool, making a mental note that she should get the sweeper going the next day and add chlorine.

She grimaced, thinking that she hadn't spent much time lately in the water. And then her grimace became a grin because she realized that the best thing to do to tire herself out a little and forget about Kane Montgomery would be to plunge into the pool. It was after eleven o'clock, but she hadn't been night swimming in ages, and it certainly was warm enough.

She hurried back to her room, changed into a sleek black one-piece suit, grabbed a massive beach towel and her terry-cloth robe, and headed back through the game room.

She paused to gaze at the pool table and remember Kane's prowess there. "One day I'll beat you at that game," she muttered aloud. "I'll beat you at all your damn games!"

And then she wondered if she wasn't going swimming simply because she hoped he would come home soon and

86

join her. She had felt so restless since he had left, so on fire.

Because he had said that they were going to go to bed together? Or because he had said that he was going to marry her?

She inhaled and exhaled deeply as she walked out onto the patio and stared into the water. Why did he have the power to make her so mad yet useless to resist him? He really was crazy if he thought he could decide just like that to marry her; he hardly knew her! And the worst of it was that he was right about her: She did want him. It was almost as if she were anticipating him, as if she had wanted to dispense with the "games" as much as he did. . . .

She made a clean dive into the water. The chill gave her body a definite little shock, but she remained below the surface, easily swimming the length of the pool.

It wasn't until she reached the shallow end that she had a thought that sent her quickly to the surface, gasping for breath.

The ranch!

Oh, God, she thought feverishly, did he want the ranch? He had come riding in just in time to save her—and it—from Ken Lander. He'd been determined to help her keep the place, and it was obvious he sure as hell didn't need a job, not to survive anyway. And he was very determined to keep the ranch going.

But it didn't make any sense. There wasn't anything that special about the Four-Leaf Clover. It was good property, it had a lot of beauty and a really fine house, but it was really special to her only because it had belonged to her family for so long—

"Were you waiting up for me?"

His low drawl brought Martie spinning around. He was down at the deep end of the pool, still in a plaid shirt and jeans, grinning tauntingly with his arms crossed over his chest and his eyes seeming to catch the moon's glitter as if they belonged to a true demon.

She watched him for a long moment, straightening her shoulders and rising in the water. "Maybe I was," she replied coolly.

Kane caught the tone of her voice and raised a brow slightly. She said nothing else, and he shrugged. "Is the hired hand allowed to join you?"

"Please do," she said dryly, crossing her arms over her chest. So far, so good. She was irritated and certainly composed enough to do battle with him.

But he immediately put a dent in her composure as he started unbuttoning his shirt. His eyes were locked with hers, and Martine managed to meet his gaze until he started to undo his belt buckle.

"I wasn't talking about skinny-dipping!" she snapped. "Please don't tell me you can't afford to have a bathing suit!"

He laughed, and she was very aware then that he was purposely trying to upset her. "Oh, I have one. Several, actually. It's just that it would take so much time . . ." He paused, sitting on one of the lounges to pull off his boots and his socks.

"No skinny-dipping!" Martine reasserted firmly.

"I wasn't planning on it," he told her, standing to shed his jeans. Naked except for his briefs, he walked to the edge and plunged in. She watched his body, lean, sinewed, and dark in the bright aqua light of the pool, as he repeated her earlier performance, propelled himself smoothly to the shallow end, and rose right before her. The moonlight caught his shoulders, and they shone with droplets of water, very broad for all that he appeared so tall and lean. His chest was thickly covered with short dark hairs that narrowed to a neat line and disappeared at the waistline of his briefs.

Martie quickly turned her eyes to his. "You could have taken the time to change," she said tersely.

He smiled. "Am I that tempting?"

"That insufferable!" she retorted, swimming away to put some distance between them. But the water was still over her head, so she backed herself against the poolside to grip the inner tile frame with her fingers while she idly treaded water.

He swam to her and watched her curiously as he hovered before her, staying afloat with very little effort.

"I wish you'd keep your distance," she said flatly.

"Oh, God!" He groaned. "What is this? Your touch-me-touch-me-not mood?" He scowled suddenly. "I think I like you better inebriated."

"You probably do," she said agreeably. She braced herself against the wall, then used her feet for a firm push and went gliding out again. But before she could reach the other side, she felt a strong tug on her foot. She twisted furiously, but the movement sent her straight into his arms, and she had no choice but to flounder there, treading the water quickly with her feet brushing his.

"What now, Martine?" he demanded harshly. "Races? Tag? Don't try it. I can beat you every time."

"But you don't play games, do you?" she inquired heatedly.

"That's right," he replied, his voice lowering in warning. "So I ask you again, what is this? You invite me in and then start with the princess routine. What's up?"

"Why do you want my ranch?" she asked abruptly, her hand brushing his chest as she raised it to smooth hair and water from her brow.

Later, and much too late, she would wonder if he hadn't hesitated too long.

But at that moment all she saw was his dark scowl and the way that his lashes fell over his glittering eyes, then lifted again with flurry of sparks that seemed to radiate a quivering heat straight into her limbs.

"Your ranch?" He spit the words out. Suddenly she found that he was swimming and that she was being swept back against a wall, cornered there by his body, his chest against hers, his arms, taut and sinewed, forming bars at her sides.

"Who in bloody hell would want your poor excuse of a ranch?" he demanded. "Broken fences, no cattle to speak of, and an old house that probably needs half a dozen renovations if it's going to stand another five years?" His voice was harsh and ridiculing; his eyes seemed to pinion her with greater power than the strength of his body. Martie longed to take back the words, but she couldn't, so she forced herself to raise her chin slightly.

"You seem to be putting a lot into such a wreck of a place," she told him.

He moved closer. She could feel the strength of his thighs against hers, hard and bare, and she swallowed uneasily because she responded so quickly to him. She could feel her nipples swell and harden as his chest rubbed against her. And his hips . . .

His briefs left very little to her imagination. There just wasn't enough clothing between them. She could feel him like a blazing fire, hard and sure and warm.

Yet he hardly seemed aware of it in his anger.

"Dammit!" he said, flaring at her. "I'm trying to help you!"

"Why?" she gasped with one last, valiant effort.

"Why?" He shook his head in confusion, and his lips formed a rueful smile. "How much more honest can I be?" he asked. "Because I want you, because I'm fascinated by you, because—"

He broke off, swiftly lowered his head, and took her lips with his. The kiss was not a tender brush this time, nor was it at all slow. It was as if he were plundering and

90

reaping from already charted waters. Passion exploded as his mouth consumed hers with a hunger and longing that left her shaking. She clung to him, feeling the full force of his body against hers. Rivulets of fire seemed to race along the length of her where his body touched hers. Her fingers tangled into the ends of his wet hair, trembled when they fell to his shoulders, and felt the heat of his flesh, the motion of the muscles beneath. He held them to the wall with one hand as he continued endlessly to drink of her lips. His free hand cupped her cheek, followed the line of her throat, then fell between them to cradle her breast, to knead it with his palm, as if testing that firmness had been a desire he could no longer resist.

She gasped deep in her throat when his hand moved again, boldly curving over her hip, slipping beneath her suit at her thigh. His lips moved from hers to nip lightly at her throat as he continued his aggressive seduction, caressing her intimately with a fluid movement that left her both stunned and quivering with need.

"Stop!" she cried at last, and he did, chuckling, catching her lips again briefly. Then he planted his hands on the edge of the pool and hoisted himself out.

He turned back to her, bending to offer her a hand. "This is it, Martine," he whispered huskily.

She stared at him for several seconds, and in all her life she would never know if she had given him her hand of her own volition or if he had hypnotized her into doing so.

She gave him her hand. He caught the other, and before she was really aware of it, she was out of the water and his arm was around her. He was staring down at her as he led her toward the bath that led to his room.

It was pitch-dark in the bedroom. He didn't seem to need light. He walked swiftly through the bath; she could feel all the tension in his arm, could hear the pad of his feet against the tiles.

"We're dripping wet" was all she could think to say.

"We'll dry," he said gruffly. But as they passed through the bath he quickly snatched a towel from the rack.

In the bedroom he turned her to face him, and his fingers slipped beneath the straps of her suit. He peeled it from her body with ease, and she could allow him to do so because it was dark and because . . . she already felt as if she were his. It was as if the moment had been preordained since she had first met him, standing there in the sunlight, a stranger yet a friend.

She closed her eyes, then felt the brush of the towel against her flesh. He was drying her, and even that simple act took on an erotic appeal. He moved the terry cloth gently over her throat, over her breasts, down to her abdomen and over the length of her legs, then between her thighs until she gasped lightly, because everywhere he touched her with the towel, he followed with the touch of his calloused fingers and the promise of his velvet lips.

The darkness swirled around her deliciously, casting her into a realm of pleasure so intense that it was almost pain. She found his hair and tugged against it, and when he held her, she found herself bolder than she might have ever imagined. She pressed against him, fusing to him, melding with him, needing him with an intensity that amazed her. Slipping her hands around his neck, she brought his head to hers and kissed him almost savagely, giving her fingers free roam of his back, lightly raking her nails along his spine and buttocks. His groans of pleasure added fuel to the soaring fire of her hunger, and she found herself nipping lightly against his throat, exploring him eagerly with her palms and fingertips, gasping slightly against his throat when she touched the full potency of his desire.

He whispered something against her ear, grazing the lobe with his teeth, and then she was lifted and the softness of the mattress was greeting her . . . and him. She felt the weight of his body, and it seemed glorious; she loved the texture of his hair-roughened legs against her, the strength of his knees, driving hers apart. She reached up to touch his cheek, and it seemed that just as the clouds had brought shadow that afternoon, the moon suddenly rose to a new peak to bring light to the room.

His features were dark with his desire; his shoulders gleamed. His eyes were still like those of a demon, yet they shone as much with tenderness as they did with deviltry.

"Kane . . ." she whispered.

He lowered his lips against hers, lightly, and stared at her in the moonlight as if sensing that she still needed assurances. "I have never wanted anything in my life as I want you," he said.

She smiled. "For the moment?" she asked wistfully.

For always, he thought. And he meant it. He had never seen eyes so beautifully wide and trusting, nor had he ever been more beguiled by a spill of hair floating like silk over a pillow, becoming entangled with his fingers. She was soft and firm beneath him; she had touched him with hunger and awe. Wherever his body had craved her, she had come with her caress.

And even now he could feel the undulation of her hips beneath him, sweetly rhythmic, like a haunting melody that drew him closer, mesmerizing and spellbinding.

He slid his hands along her back to the curve of her buttocks and lifted her, bringing her to meet his thrust. A little sound escaped her, and she clung to him. He held still, letting her absorb him, kissing her lightly, then deeply plunging his tongue into her mouth along with the thrust of his body.

He took care with her, gentle care, tender care, until her thrusts rose to meet his, and then something somewhere inside him exploded with a wild magic. His desire riddled through him like drumbeats, a thundering pulse that ruled his body. She was a blaze that embraced and welcomed him and urged him ever onward. Onward, reaching for a climax that rent him again and again as waves of release washed through him with a splendor that consumed his soul. Vaguely he heard her cry out with a sweet, wondering ecstasy all her own, and he pulled her into his arms, spent and shaken by the brilliance of their passion.

Long moments later he felt her shift and realized his weight was still on her. He quickly moved over to her side and raised himself on an elbow to see her in the darkness. She was still breathing heavily, and a glimmer of perspiration made her breasts catch the moon's reflection as they rose and fell. Fascinated all over again, he cupped one firm mound in his hand.

His eyes met hers again. She curled against him.

"Who are you really, Kane?"

"Does it matter?" he asked, smoothing her damp hair from her cheek, running his knuckles lightly over the softness of her flesh.

"Yes," she whispered.

"I'm the man who's falling in love with you. The man who's in love with you. The man who's going to marry you."

She smiled at him and touched the cleft in his jaw. "This isn't the Wild West, partner," she drawled softly. "You don't have to marry the lady just because you've stolen her virtue."

"I didn't steal anything; it was given to me," he told her. "And I do have to marry the lady . . . because she's mine." He kissed her forehead, her nose, her lips. "Because I'm hers."

And then he balanced himself above her again, drawn by the wide splendor of her eyes. "I didn't hurt you, did I?"

She shook her head no.

He suddenly felt himself grow tense with newfound anger. "I swear if I ever see Ken Lander near you again, he won't be able to walk away."

Martie shivered a little at the intensity of his words.

"Oh, my God," he murmured suddenly, vehemently, burying his face against her hair and holding her tight. "I've never felt anything like this. . . ."

She smiled, feeling an electric thrill race through her from the beauty of his words. "Really?" she murmured.

"Really."

He looked at her again, grinning like a schoolboy. "All mine, only mine!" he said teasingly.

"Do men always get so possessive?"

He shrugged. "I don't know. I've never felt possessive before. But right now I feel like Christopher Columbus—sailing uncharted waters and making the discovery of a lifetime. Only this is a discovery I intend to see remains charted by one man—one man alone."

She stared at him, and her smile faded as she grew curious. "How can you know that you love me, Kane?"

"I just do. And I know now that you have the same feelings, the same intensity, or you would never have been with me tonight."

She flushed a little because she couldn't deny his words. That she had been overwhelmed by him was obvious. That she never done anything like this before was equally obvious.

But she shook her head, and she spoke in a whisper. "You still haven't answered me, Kane. Who are you?"

He grinned. "Marry me, Martie. Find out over the years and years it takes to live out a lifetime."

"You're crazy."

"I'm serious."

"You can't be!"

"I am."

"Kane—"

95

"All right." He sighed with resignation and drew his finger slowly over her collarbone, then down between the valley of her breasts. He leaned over her, and against her lips he whispered, "Then I'll have to settle for another . . . trial run, my love."

Within seconds she was far too breathless to argue that proposal.

CHAPTER FIVE

"Let's not go to Joe's tonight," Kane said suddenly.

They had been companionably silent for so long that Martine jumped at the sound of his voice. It had been a little more than a week since the first night she had shared with him, and she mused now that though she knew him with a wonderful intimacy, he still kept a lot of his thoughts to himself and was therefore able to startle her when he did speak suddenly.

She realized, too, that the ranch had never run so smoothly. In fact, everything in her life seemed smooth and incredible, as if she were living among the clouds.

Martie didn't always know where Kane was since he had a habit of disappearing at the strangest times, yet she felt little jealousy. Perhaps it was because when they were alone he had such a talent for making her feel as if she were beautiful and unique, the most important person in the world to him.

He could also make her laugh easily, and once she had started laughing, he could sober her just as quickly, sweeping her at will into a whirlwind of passion and desire. . . .

"Hey!" He nudged her lightly. "Are you paying any attention to me, Ms. Galway? I said, let's skip Joe's. I can give him a call and beg out of the evening."

It was lunchtime, and they were sitting by the brook. Kane was resting against a tree; Martine was situated

97

between his knees, resting her head against his chest. It was a beautiful place to be. She felt very content and lazy, and very loved, just leaning against him and staring up at the dark patterns the leaves were creating against the sky.

"Why not?" she asked, twisting her head to look up at him.

He was staring out at the plain, idly chewing on a blade of grass and lightly stroking her arm.

"I think we should do something alone. Go out, have dinner, get married."

Martine laughed. He gazed down at her, smiling. She liked the soft golden glow in his eyes.

"You're crazy!" she exclaimed. "You don't really know me—"

"I know everything I need to know," he said determinedly.

"But I still don't know anything about you!"

"Don't you?" he said lightly, and she found herself blushing because physically there wasn't much she didn't know about him now.

"I don't know when your birthday is; I don't know how old you are, I don't know where you come from. I don't know if you hate your brother or if you even have a brother."

"I have two of them and I love them both. If you were to marry me, you'd find out my age and my birth date— I'd have to fill them in on the license. Let me see . . . both my parents are living; they're healthy, normal people with no serious complexes that I know about. I like big breakfasts, beer, and I admit to a bad temper at times. I don't drink too much, I don't gamble too much, and there's no record of lunacy in the family tree. I pick up after myself, I can use both a washer and dryer, and I can cook."

"You're perfect!" Martie laughed, nuzzling her forehead against his chin.

"So grab me—quickly," he told her.

"Hmm. You're just a little too perfect," she murmured, adding tauntingly, "The strong, silent type. Too silent."

"Oh, no." He groaned. "Not that again!"

"You are serious, aren't you?" she asked, twisting around to stare up into his eyes. He nodded slowly with a rueful grin, and she felt a little thrill race through her. Could he really, really be in love with her? Feeling the same forever fascination that burned in her heart whenever she gazed his way?

She tried to steady the soaring excitement that raced through her and closed her eyes to lie against his shoulder again. What did *she* feel? He had taken her so completely by storm, surely her emotions were reeling with the sheer physical impact he had had upon her. Nothing in her life had prepared her for Kane. Their nights together had been like roller-coaster rides, shatteringly skyrocketing her again and again to realms of a heaven she had never imagined could exist. Was she so beguiled by him that she couldn't think or feel straight?

It was possible, she told herself firmly, but there had been more than the volatile passion and excitement. Martie instinctively knew that she could not have found a more tender lover, a more gentle tutor. He could be highly aggressive, but he could as easily draw back to lead her along.

She had worried once that he would leave her, but now he wanted to marry her. In all her life she had never met a man like Kane. It was doubtful if she would ever do so again. He wanted to bind their lives together. If she gave him up . . .

She stared up at him again. "Kane, what's the need to rush? I know I don't want to lose you, but it's just so sudden that it's—crazy!"

He laughed, tossing the blade of grass away. He bent down to kiss her passionately, his hand savoring the fullness of her breast as his lips coerced hers with a thrilling heat.

And when he broke away, his mouth remained close to hers. "You're the reason," he whispered. "What's between us is the reason. I can't let you go, Martie. I want you bound to me in every way possible. I want you to love me, I want you to be my wife. I want you to bear my name and our children and everything else. And if another man even gazed at you too long, I think I'd go a little insane."

She swallowed, aware of the vehemence of his whisper. She was in love with him, she realized fully. Fascinated . . . and in love. If he were to walk away from her now, she would ache as if she had lost part of herself. He had rescued her, he had awakened her—and she was far more his than she wanted him to know.

She tried to offer him a taunting grin. "Do you propose often?"

"I've never proposed before in my life."

"But you've had lots of affairs, haven't you?"

He shrugged, holding her close. "A share, I suppose. That's why I know. . . . Martine, I've never felt anything like this. I want to spend my life getting to know you, everything about you, waking up with you on the pillow beside me, touching you, having you."

"It's crazy," she reiterated for what felt like the thousandth time.

He grinned. "Haven't you ever done anything crazy? Seen something you wanted and just reached to grab it?"

"No," she replied honestly. "I've never really had the time or the chance. Oh, don't get me wrong. I think I've had a lovely life! The local junior college was great, but with Mom gone, I didn't have all the free time the other kids did. I was always feeding hands, cleaning stalls, keeping the house up, and riding the old range! And then, when I lost Dad . . ." Her voice drifted away; it was still too close for her to speak without emotion, so she determined not to speak anymore.

He shifted and pulled her to him on the bed of grass beneath the tree. His eyes appeared very dark and intense when he spoke, his voice strong and warm and deeply impassioned. "Martine, you've had such a hard time. I want to make life easier for you; I want to make it fun. I want to love and cherish you and share your fights and help win your battles. Trust me. I love you."

She smiled, touching the contour of his strong jaw with wonder. "It wasn't all that bad," she said a little ruefully. "I do know how to fight by myself!"

"I know. I've seen you. But everyone needs someone on their side, Martine." He rolled onto his back and stared up at the sun. "If you're worried about the ranch," he said suddenly, a little harshly, "we can have some kind of a prenuptial document drawn up, stating that you own it entirely and always will."

She froze. "I—I'm—"

"What?"

She leaned over him, staring earnestly into his eyes. "Kane, if we were to get married, I wouldn't want any documents or legal agreements. I know it's done sometimes, but that isn't marriage to me. Marriage means forever."

He wove his fingers through her hair, pulling her closer. "Marriage is meant to be forever," he told her softly. "I mean to love you forever."

She laughed, suddenly so thrilled and excited that she was breathless. "All right, then. How about a month from today?"

He sat up abruptly and pulled her across his lap and into his arms. "What's the matter with today?"

"Today?"

"Why put it off?" he asked. "Let's elope. We can fly into Vegas for the ceremony if you like. We'll spend a

101

quick honeymoon there for the weekend and show up at Joe's for dinner Monday night as an old married couple!"

"It's insane. . . ."

"Let's do it!"

She found herself staring into the golden flames of his eyes as if hypnotized. Then she slowly nodded.

He let out something like a rebel war cry and stood with her still in his arms, laughing delightedly.

"Ms. Galway, get back to the ranch and start packing. I'll ride out and find Bill and tell him he's in charge until Monday."

He set her on her feet, turned her toward her horse, and gave her a gentle prod toward Cheyenne with a tap on her bottom.

"Give them an inch, and they think they own you!" Martine said complainingly, but her heart was racing. She was very breathless and excited and could hardly believe what she was doing.

Yet she wanted to do it. Suddenly and with all her heart she was sure. She wanted to be his wife. She wanted to live with him and grow old with him and one day share a family with him. . . . He wanted to marry her. He hadn't just wanted her. He had fallen in love with her, he did love her—and he did want to marry her.

"I haven't got a thing to wear!" she cried suddenly.

"We'll buy something," he said. "Just hurry or we'll never get a license in time. Now you have got me crazy. If you aren't Mrs. Kane Montgomery by tonight, I could wind up certifiably insane!"

To add credence to his words, he stalked quickly after her and lifted her onto the huge buckskin. "Make tracks!" he said teasingly.

She nodded, still smiling ridiculously and thinking that he was, beyond a doubt, the most striking man in the world. Tall and lean with an air of assurance that was as alluring as it was implacable.

He did have a temper, she reminded herself, shivering a little. He was still an enigma. No matter what he said, she still didn't know much about him.

But she knew she couldn't let him go. She couldn't hop off the roller coaster, not now, no matter what highs or lows the ride might be careening toward.

"Are you going to tell Bill what we're doing?" she asked curiously, smiling slightly at the demon's gleam of mischief that touched his eyes.

"Uh-uh. We'll make it a complete surprise."

She laughed. "And they will be surprised, Mr. Montgomery. In company you've been entirely circumspect. I don't think any of them suspect that you—that we've—"

"Been sleeping together?" he said. "Don't count on that, Ms. Galway. You've had a nice, contented sparkle in your eyes lately."

"Have I?" Martine retorted. "And you consider yourself responsible. Arrogant as always!"

"Not arrogant, Martine. Aware, that's all. Now get going!"

"Don't think you're going to spend a lifetime ordering me around!" she told him, but she wasn't sure he heard the entire warning. He had given Cheyenne a good smack on the rump, and the buckskin had responded to him just as quickly as she was prone to do. Cheyenne even seemed to know exactly where they were going; he galloped eagerly toward the barn.

It was where he was fed, she reminded herself. Most horses were eager to head back to their stalls and pasture. . . . But she still couldn't quite shake the feeling that Kane could even will the buckskin to do his bidding.

In the house she tried to make herself pause and consider what she was about to do. But even as she tried to force practicality into her thoughts, she quickly showered. Then she pulled out her newest dress, a watery green sleeveless silk with a mandarin collar and a skirt that was hemmed just above her knees and swirled with a pleasant rhythm when she walked.

She pushed the bathroom door closed to stare into the full-length mirror attached to it and surveyed herself critically.

The silk was such a soft color that the green did not clash with the vibrant streaks of red in her hair, which she left free, the ends curling just over her shoulders. The simple hairstyle went well with the mandarin collar. She thought she looked just a little too thin and a little too pale. But the soft green did pick up the bright color of her eyes; enhanced by the gown, they seemed a deep kelly shade, almost as dark as a forest.

She looked frightened, she decided, and lightly slapped her cheeks to bring some color to them. She still looked frightened. Not frightened—nervous. Brides were supposed to be nervous, weren't they?

She heard a long, low whistle behind her and raised her eyes slightly, catching Kane's in the mirror. He smiled at her, and her heart fluttered.

"I'll change quickly," he said, turning away to head down the hall.

Martine raced to the doorway after him. "Kane!"

He paused, gazing at her with a curious smile.

"Are we really doing this?"

A grin split across his features, forming a myriad of tiny lines about his eyes.

"Really," he told her, and turned again.

Martine threw things haphazardly into a suitcase, then paced the living room as she waited for him, feeling as if she were suffering the effects of some kind of drug.

But ten minutes later, when he came for her, she stood still, staring at him. He was in an expertly tailored three-piece navy suit, a vested garment that accentuated the breadth of his shoulder and leanness of his hips. His hair was damp, as dark as ebony, and his eyes were gleaming devilishly once more. He came up to her to reach for her hands, and she noted the spattering of dark hair on the broad backs of his hands. He dipped his head down to kiss her, and she inhaled the shower freshness of him and felt dizzy all over again.

"Let's go."

The truck took them as far as the airport; they were flying straight to Las Vegas. On the plane Kane suggested dryly that she might want to order a drink. Martine shook her head.

"If I'm going to do something this insane," she murmured, "I'm going to do it completely sober!"

By four o'clock they were filling out their license application. Martine started laughing nervously, and Kane demanded to know why.

"It's true. I finally know something about you." She indicated the paper he was filling out. "You're only thirty-three?"

He gave her a slightly evil glare. "Are you saying I'm aging badly?"

She laughed. "No, not really. You just have—"

"I suggest you say I have an air of maturity," he said dryly. "That way we can at least save the first squabble for after the ceremony!"

"Okay, it's an air of maturity," she said agreeably.

Kane paced while they waited for the processing of the license; Martine wondered if he was getting his own case of the jitters.

"You can always back out," she told him softly.

He stopped and stared at her. "What?"

"I said you can always back out of this."

He laughed. "Are you crazy? I want them to hurry—before *you* think too much and decide you want to back out." He took a seat beside her, cupped her cheek gently, and studied her eyes. "Rich and lush and verdent like an endless field," he murmured. Then he brushed her lips with a kiss and grinned. "I couldn't get you pliably tipsy on the plane, so I have to take my chances with your rational mind."

She returned his stare, hoping with all her heart that the tenderness she read in his warm golden gaze was real.

"I have no rational mind when I'm with you," she said honestly.

He started to put his arms around her, but just then the clerk called them, and they had the license in their hands.

Before Martine knew it, she was out on the street, being dragged along. "Where are we going?"

"The first place I can find!" He laughed.

And it wasn't ten minutes later that they were standing before a justice of the peace. A sudden and very serious case of shivers suddenly overwhelmed her; she was among total strangers, making the most important commitment of her life.

Kane stated his vows strongly and with no hesitancy. Martine tried to say, "I do," and nothing came out. She had to wet her lips and try again, and the vow came out very weakly.

She had no ring for him, and in the middle of the service she wondered when he had gotten a ring for her. But he had. It was a wide etched gold band, and it slid a little too easily onto her finger. While the service continued she stupidly stood there thinking that she would have to get the ring sized.

And then Kane was kissing her. She realized that it was over, that they were married.

The justice who had married them was asking for her signature; his witness was smiling and passing them token glasses of champagne. Plastic glasses, Martine thought a little hysterically. She drank the champagne in one swallow.

Kane paid the justice, and then they were out on the street again. Dusk was just starting to fall.

"Hello, Mrs. Montgomery," Kane said a little huskily. "Are you with us?"

She nodded. "I—I just don't believe it. I think I'm still in shock. I'm supposed to be at dinner at a neighbor's, and I just got married instead. I did it entirely of my own volition—and I still don't believe I did it."

He laughed, and his voice lowered against her ear. "I'm very, very real, Mrs. Montgomery. Want me to prove it?"

She looked up at him, but his gaze was already on the street. He was hailing a taxi.

"Where are we going?" she asked.

He chuckled. "To consummate the marriage, of course."

"It was consummated before the fact!" Martine protested quietly, very aware of the cabdriver.

He pulled her close to him in the cab, gave the driver the name of their hotel, and whispered, "I've never, ever made love to my wife before."

But at the hotel there was little choice except to wait. Their room wasn't quite ready. The concierge was very apologetic, explaining that they'd been given very short notice. Kane accepted the news with a shrug.

He took her to one of the dining rooms, a quiet place with no stage show, only very soft piano music. The lighting was subdued, and they were led to a booth with comfortable leather seats. They faced each other for the meal, and when Kane ordered a very expensive bottle of champagne to start, Martine was careful not to lift a brow.

She waited until they were served. She'd crossed her legs beneath the table and discreetly tossed off a sandal so she could run her stockinged toes along his ankle. She swirled her champagne in the glass, watching him above

107

its rim. He was smiling slightly, as if he were expecting a third degree.

"Okay, Mr. Montgomery," she drawled softly. "Where did you get your money?"

His lashes fell slightly, and his lips twisted with amusement. "I earned it, Mrs. Montgomery. And invested it wisely."

"On loans like mine?" she asked skeptically.

"Don't ever knock the small businessman—"

"Woman," she interjected politely, "I'm a business-woman."

"Don't knock them, either sex," he told her. "Yes, I've made a lot of loans. A lot like yours. Except you can rip up that paper now, you know."

She sipped her champagne and appreciated the very smooth tickle that touched her nose and cooled her throat. "I want to repay the loan. Loans, actually. I want to prove that the ranch can do it."

He shrugged without arguing, but she knew he had no intention of keeping business separate.

Martine felt she should argue the question now. But then she decided not to. She had married him, and she had been the one to say that she didn't believe in prenuptial agreements. If she was going to marry a man, she was going to do it all the way.

"No strings attached," she murmured.

"What?" he asked, arching a brow and gazing at her in a way that subtly declared she was a little crazy.

"Nothing. Now—"

"Now?"

"Let's back up a little bit. You made most of your money from investments—"

"And bank robbery, of course."

"Kane!"

He sighed, amused, exasperated. "Stocks, for one. Land, for another. All legit."

"What are your brother's names?"

He laughed. "Michael Pierson Montgomery and Evan Taylor Montgomery. Michael is the oldest; Evan, the baby. But don't tell him that—he's twenty-six and heartily resents any such terminology. Neither of them is a bank robber either."

"Your father?"

"No, Dad isn't a bank robber either."

"What's his name?" Martie asked, refusing to smile.

"Michael Peter. My mother's name is Catherine. Catherine Mary. She was a Taylor. That's where Evan got his middle name."

"Do you all get along?"

"Quite well. We spent a few years tearing one another's hair out, as I hear siblings are prone to do, but we're rather supportive these days."

"School?"

"Yes, ma'am. I went." He was teasing her. Her eyes narrowed, and he rattled off his high school and his Arizona college. Then he told her, "If this is twenty questions, you're running out."

She laughed. "Oh, no! You promised—"

"I did." He sighed. "Go on."

"Your family is well-off?"

"Quite comfortable."

"And your parents—"

"Are very nice people. You'll meet them soon."

"When?"

"When we've had a little time alone."

She opened her mouth again, and he laughed. "What? What? We're going to be married a lifetime, you know. You don't have to ask every single question tonight."

Martine shook her head. She was suddenly longing to reach out and touch the fabric of his jacket and then to stroke his cheek. He looked so wonderful in his suit. And then she was also thinking that he looked wonderful

109

without any outfit and that she had married him! It was her absolute right to want to touch him, and it was a feeling that made her smile with satisfaction.

He caught her hand across the table. "What's that smirk for?"

"All good things," she told him lightly.

"Oh, yeah?"

"Mmm . . ." She leaned over the table slightly, bringing her head closer to his. "I was just thinking that I've seen half a dozen women stripping you with their eyes tonight, and I was feeling ridiculously pleased because I'm the only one who gets to do it in the flesh."

"I do like that," he told her huskily. Then he laughed. "It makes me feel a little primitive, though. I've seen several men looking at you the same way, and it makes me feel like I'd like to flatten them if they took a step too close."

"Possessive, eh?" she asked teasingly.

He sipped his champagne, watching her. "I warned you about that from the very beginning." He smiled. "Want to order?"

They both decided on the chef's specialty, a fillet of fish cooked with herbs. Their conversation became very light, with Kane giving her a wild discourse on his life, telling her his preference of player's piece for the game Monopoly, that he loved water, dogs, and horses, hated tennis, and loved golf.

"What about your parents?" Martie asked. "Won't they be a little shocked to learn they have a daughter-in-law?"

He merely shrugged. "Nothing I do ever shocks them. My mother will be thrilled to death—trust me. She's been after me for at least ten years now to settle down."

Martine felt light—light and free and happier and dizzier than she had ever been in her life. They followed the meal with Sambuca and rum cake, then idly wandered

110

into one of the casinos. The one-armed bandits caught her attention, and Kane, in an incredibly amiable mood, smiled and left her for a moment, only to return with a handful of silver dollars.

The money had a touch of the unreal, of the magical, just like the night. She could do no wrong with it. Kane's hand was lightly on her back as she played the machine, laughing almost hysterically when she hit two jackpots in a row.

"And to think that not two weeks ago I was on the verge of ruin!" she said, leaning back against his jacket, tired and contented yet keyed up with a delightful energy.

"Feast or famine," Kane said dryly. "Well, I think you've about cleaned this lady out. I also think we should have a room by now!"

They had a room all right. Martine decided she knew what had taken so long. It was a beautifully and elaborately appointed suite with roses everywhere, baskets of cheeses and fruits, and ice buckets holding the same champagne they had enjoyed in the dining room.

Still the most breath-catching appeal of the room was the glass doors, open to the night and a cool breeze, that looked out across a wrought-iron balcony to the myriad lights all around them. It was a kaleidoscope of color, but the room was also situated for privacy, so that one could see out yet not be seen.

Martine was drawn to the open doors. She heard Kane tip the bellboy with a friendly comment, and then the door closed. She smiled, closing her eyes. She could, concentrating on the effort, hear his smooth footsteps until she felt his hands on her shoulders, pulling her against him.

She spun around and rubbed her cheek against his jacket, then slipped her fingers around his neck and looked into his eyes.

111

"I think you must be a cattle rustler," she told him.

He gave her his elusive grin, winding his arms around her and smoothing his palms over the small of her back, pulling her hard against him.

"There's only one thing about me that should concern you at this moment," he answered.

"Oh?"

"Yes. The fact that I am your newly wed husband and that you're just dying to get your hands on me."

She laughed, feeling the effects of the champagne ever more strongly in his arms. His fingers moved along her spine, finding the zipper to her gown and lowering it very slowly. He slipped the gown over her shoulders and watched the silk fall to her feet. Then he lowered his head to her shoulder. He kissed it, grazing it lightly with his teeth, and she cast back her head, moaning softly at the jolt of liquid heat that raced through her. Her fingers tangled his dark hair, and she murmured, "Oh, Kane, I do love you so much. Please, please, be real!"

She thought he stiffened just a bit, but maybe it was the champagne. A second later it didn't matter because he had found the hook to her bra and released it, and all she could think about was the sensation of his hand caressing her, teasing her nipple to an erotic peak. She caught his face and kissed him and demanded the right to help him shed his coat and his vest and shirt. . . .

Soon they both were naked, warm where they touched each other, cool where the breeze blew around them. But when he lifted her in his arms, he didn't take her to bed. He carried her into the bathroom, where there was there a huge oval tub spilling over with bubbles—and sporting ice buckets of champagne at each end. Martine giggled delightedly, surprised that such a rugged man would give way to such whimsy, yet thrilled that he had.

He set her carefully into the tub, then crawled in beside her. She started to reach for the champagne.

"Not yet," he told her huskily, and her eyes widened, for he was rising over her, catching her lips, pushing her knees apart with his own. She gasped with pure ecstasy when he moved into her with a swift thrust. She saw the glitter of his golden eyes and was thrilled, quivering as he held there, then demanding that he move. . . .

And when it was over, she was stunned again by the incredibly wonderful way it was possible to feel. Like a star in the heavens, like the sun, like a being composed of the sweetest nectar . . .

"Oh, Kane!" Delightfully sated and lazy, she slipped her arms around his neck and leaned against him, reveling in the warm water about her and the feel of his body next to hers.

He shifted slightly, holding her while he poured out a glass of champagne for them to share.

"Mmm," she murmured, taking a sip and leaning against his chest. "Mr. Montgomery, you do know how to do a honeymoon right. I feel so . . . wonderfully, wonderfully weary!"

"Don't get too weary on me, Mrs. Montgomery. We've just begun," he whispered to her. He kissed her, and she tasted the champagne on his lips, and in a few minutes she learned that he didn't say things that he didn't entirely mean.

The night had just begun.

The honeymoon had just begun. The two days that followed were the best time Martie had ever had. They gambled; they swam; despite his disclaimers, they hit the tennis courts. Martine even learned the basics of golf.

She had known before that Kane knew how to work; now she learned that he knew how to play. They ate breakfast in bed, had lunch by the pool, and made love at any time.

It very simply was the best time of her life. She'd never felt more cherished or loved.

And she reflected, lying awake near dawn on the morning they were to leave, she had never thought it was possible to love someone so fiercely in return.

If she still felt that she didn't really know everything she should about him, she had all the time in the world in which to learn. Love was this wonder, this experiencing. It was also learning to live together. And she told herself vehemently, it was trusting in the man she loved.

Staring at the slightly loose gold band on her finger, she curled more tightly against her husband. She had promised to love him. And if she loved him, she would give him her trust until he was ready to divulge more about himself.

CHAPTER SIX

There were flowers on her dresser when she awoke in her own bed on Monday morning. They were the first thing that Martine saw, and she smiled and stretched luxuriously and closed her eyes once again. Her fingers smoothed over the pillow beside her where Kane had slept, and she decided with contentment that she loved being a wife.

Seconds later she opened her eyes again, then blinked quickly to focus on the bedside clock. It was almost one in the afternoon.

Martine bounded out of bed and into the shower. When she dressed and went into the kitchen, she was surprised to find Sonia there, humming away while she stirred chili in a big pot.

Sonia gave her a tremendous smile. "Morning, Mrs. Montgomery!" Then she dropped the wooden spoon and rushed over to give Martine a warm and slightly teary hug. "Oh, honey, I'm so very, very happy for you."

Martine chuckled and then discovered that her own eyes were a little damp. Smiling, she held herself away from Sonia. "I take it Kane gave you the news."

"He certainly did!" Sonia winked. "And he said not to wake you either, that you didn't have much sleep over the weekend."

Martie flushed slightly and walked over to the stove. "The chili smells great. Have you got coffee going?"

"Sure thing!"

Martine poured herself a cup of coffee and sat at the kitchen table with it. Sonia chatted on cheerfully about how sorry she was to have missed the wedding, but then an elopement could be very romantic.

"And your daddy would have been so very happy to see you with a man like that!"

Martine sipped her coffee thoughtfully. "Do you really think so, Sonia?"

"Would I say so if I didn't?"

Martie hesitated for a moment, giving herself a little shake and wondering why she was suddenly feeling unsure. "Sonia, you're not, uh, surprised that it's all happened so fast?"

"Well, I've always believed that what's right is right and what's wrong can never be righted by time. You two just kind of have a thing about you. You did from the very start." Sonia was stirring the chili again. She paused, her hand on her hip, and stared into space for a moment, then shrugged. "There's no way to explain love or people. I don't know exactly how you tell, but there's something about that man that's just as right as rain."

Martie stood up, glad that Sonia's instincts were the same as her own. She'd felt the strangest qualm sitting there drinking her coffee. It made no sense. She'd married Kane stone-cold sober because she'd wanted to; their brief honeymoon and return home had been bliss. Now, suddenly, she was frightened. It made no sense.

Martine set her coffee cup slowly in the sink, then turned back to Sonia. "Thanks for letting me sleep this morning. I guess I did need it. But, Sonia, do me a favor. Don't let me make a habit out of sleeping all morning, okay?"

Sonia shrugged. "If you ask me, Martine, you two should still be off somewhere. A two-day honeymoon, what's that?" She sniffed audibly.

"Well," Martine murmured, "we can plan something longer somewhere along the line." She paused. "Where's Kane?"

"Said this morning that he was going out to the cliffs to try to trap that mountain cat."

"Thanks. I think I'll go find him," Martine said cheerfully. She hurried to the door, but Sonia called her back.

"Martie, I forgot to tell you. You're going to the senator's for dinner at eight. Kane gave him the news, and he's planning a small get-together."

"Okay," Martine said. Then she asked curiously, "By the way, what's going on here? How come you're in the kitchen and I could sleep all morning?"

Sonia laughed. "It's just because everything's really under control. Things are going smoothly, honey. You'll just have to get used to it!"

Martine gave Sonia a weak smile and departed the kitchen, wondering again just what was the matter with her. She was married to a man she loved—even if he did still seem to be a bit of a stranger.

As she saddled Cheyenne she admitted to herself that she was a little jealous. She'd been struggling to get by, then along came Kane, and everything was suddenly easy. Maybe she felt she was losing her grip on things that were rightfully hers. After all, the Four-Leaf Clover was her ranch. Or was it? She had been the one to say that she didn't believe in prenuptial agreements. If she were going to marry, it would be with the determination that the commitment was forever. And that made the Four-Leaf Clover Kane's property too. She should be thrilled that he could do so well with it.

It was a long ride out to the cliffs, and by the time she reached them and started up one of the narrow dirt trails, she and Cheyenne both were soaked with sweat from the heat of the afternoon sun. Maybe coming out here had been a bad idea, Martine reflected. Surely, if Kane were only setting a trap, he would be through by now. She'd probably taken the long ride for nothing.

Curving through a path hewn between high rock boulders and small caves, Cheyenne suddenly stumbled. Cursing softly beneath her breath, Martine dismounted and had to dig in her pocket for a pick to clean out his hoof. She sighed a little with relief when she found the offending stone, but while she was at her task the horse sneezed, consequently resoaking her back.

"Ugh! You lowlife!" she said to the horse. "Honestly, try to help someone—even a horse—and . . ."

Her voice trailed away as she noticed a small cascade of dust and stones falling onto one of the boulders about twenty feet away. Looking up and shielding her eyes from the sun with her hand, she thought she saw something.

"Come on, horse," she told Cheyenne. "Let's make tracks."

She led him upward along the trail. Reaching the barren patch of dust above the boulder, she found Kane's big bay, Thor, stamping his feet and flicking his tail about to rid himself of annoying flies. Patting the horse, she frowned. "So he is still around somewhere, big fellow. Where?"

She hadn't really expected an answer from the horse, and she didn't get one. "All right, you two stay here," she told Thor and Cheyenne. "I'll find him myself."

She started to explore the area a little nervously. She didn't like the caves—rattlers were fond of making those cool spots their homes—and they really weren't so much caves as they were caverns, with untrustworthy roofs formed of the stone shelves that made up the cliffs.

"Kane?" Martine called out, moving up to the dark entrance of one. She hesitated, waiting for answer, then jumped and gasped out a startled scream when a hand touched her on the shoulder.

It was Kane, and he was scowling darkly. Hardly the reception she would have expected from the man she had just married.

"What are you doing here?" he demanded curtly. He was wearing a hat against the sun, the brim low over his eyes.

"Looking for you," she answered honestly, trying to study his features. Between the hat and the sun at his back she couldn't read his expression, but his tension told her he was angry, and she felt confused and suddenly very, very insecure.

"Why?"

Martine shrugged, backing slightly against the hard rock formation. "I thought I'd find you, that's all." His hands were on his hips, and he looked like a dark and dangerous shadow against the sun. "Oh, for heaven's sake!" she muttered irritably. "I didn't think it was a crime for a wife to look for her husband."

He turned suddenly and walked down to the horses, calling over his shoulder, "And I didn't think a marriage license meant a woman was supposed to keep hourly tabs on a man!"

Martie felt as if he had slapped her. Her breath sucked in with a rush as she watched his retreating back, and tears stung her eyes. She vaguely noted that he paused to grab a large pick and shovel off the ground, but then she turned in a sudden fury and walked several feet in the opposite direction to gaze out on the cactus-strewn plain far below the cliffs.

Damn him! Was the honeymoon over so soon? Was this their first marital spat? Or was it proof that she had made a rather serious mistake? "Married in haste, we may repent at leisure."

"What are you doing?" he called out impatiently.

Martine spun around, astounded by the question. "I'm staring into space!" she snapped.

119

"Well, come on. It's a long ride back."

"I know how to get there," she replied coolly. "I was the one born and raised here, you know."

His head lowered, and she thought she could hear his sigh, even from a distance.

He raised his head, pushed his hat back, and walked toward her. "Martine." He touched her shoulders; she couldn't help jerking away. "I'm sorry. It's hot out here, and it feels like it's been a long day. Can we ride back, please?"

His tone sounded more impatient than apologetic, and she still felt hurt, miserably so. It was as if now that they were back to reality, marriage had changed everything. On top of that, she was suddenly being forced to realize that she had truly just married a man she didn't know at all.

She walked past him stiffly. "Certainly."

She was mounted on Cheyenne before he reached Thor. She was tempted to race down the trail but knew that he would ridicule her because it would be an act of foolish defiance and she might hurt Cheyenne.

Martine contented herself with urging Cheyenne into a quick, long-legged walk. But she couldn't remain silent, not when she sensed that the bay was right behind her.

"I'd like to remind you, Kane, that I was in no hurry to be married."

For a long moment he didn't reply. Then he said between gritted teeth, "I said I was sorry, Martie."

" 'Sorry' doesn't take back things already said."

To that he didn't reply.

The sun was going down, but the day didn't seem to cool any. And thirty minutes later they were still riding in a miserable silence. Martine urged Cheyenne into a canter and heard the bay behind her follow suit.

She nudged Cheyenne into a gallop. Once again the bay followed suit.

All at once the breakneck pace was slowed. Kane came alongside her, grasped Cheyenne's reins, and pulled him in. Martine gave her new husband a furious glare, swearing at him as she fought to regain control of her own mount. It did no good. Both horses slowed to a halt. Then Kane was on his feet and dragging her down to hers.

"What do you think you're doing?" Martine asked heatedly. "Let go of me. Maybe the ranch became half your property, but I didn't."

"Oh, no?" he said, his eyes glittering. His hands remained locked around her waist. Martine pressed her lips together and tried to break his hold, realizing all the while that the whole thing was ridiculous yet being terrified that she was going to cry because it also seemed to be such a disaster.

"Martine, stop it!"

"You stop it! Just leave me alone."

"No. I am not going back to the house like this."

She ceased struggling, tossing back a wave of hair to stare into his eyes. "Why not? Aren't others supposed to believe that there might be trouble in paradise?"

Kane gritted his teeth together, well aware that he was in trouble. Her eyes were sparkling like an array of emeralds, and her hair had never looked wilder or redder, highlighted by the falling crimson sun.

And then he smiled as he watched her stiff and rebellious stance and the proud and determined tilt of her chin. Fire in her eyes and her hair—it was part of what had fascinated him thoroughly. Allured him and then beguiled him and bound him. Inwardly he winced, aware that he was at fault. And he couldn't think of any reason at all for jumping at her the way he had, except that she had come upon him exactly when he didn't want her to know what he was doing. He was deeply in love with her —in a way he had never thought possible—and she was his wife. But not even that could change commitments and promises already made.

"Martine," he said quietly, "you have a right to be angry. But please, let's not make a major thing out of something so ridiculous. I don't believe in quarreling like this. I love you."

She continued to stare at him with the sun's blaze in her eyes. Then she sighed, and her lashes fell like rich velvet to sweep away the defiant rage. She smiled slightly. "I'm not property, Kane Montgomery," she said regally.

He laughed. "No, you're not. I'm sorry for that too. It was just that I suddenly felt I was tangling with a wild-cat."

He wound his fingers into her hair, entranced by the sun's play on it, and bent to kiss her, slowly and deeply. Her body melded nicely with his, so nicely that he had to remind himself that they were in an open field. He whispered huskily against her lips, "I guess we'd better get back."

"Mmm," she murmured. He grazed his knuckles lightly over her cheek and shivered slightly, marveling again at the depth of his need for her and the fact that she really was his completely. His wife.

If only he could remember his dual roles for a while, he reminded himself. He hugged her more closely to him, regardless of the heat, not caring that they both were covered with prairie dust and sweat. Touching her always had a shattering effect on him, like a blade of heat raging deep inside him, making him hunger and yearn, yet making him feel the greatest swell of tenderness. And protectiveness—and possessiveness, too, he thought, smiling over her head. No, she wasn't property. But she was his, and he knew he would fight any battle to keep it that way.

"Do you forgive me?" he asked, lips nuzzling her forehead as he spoke.

"I suppose," she murmured teasingly, leaning against him with a little sigh.

"Are you sure?"

"Absolutely."

"Will you wash my back then?"

"Honestly, give a man an inch . . ." She was taunting him, raising her head to study him again. The emerald glitter was back in her eyes. But now it was an endless green beauty that beckoned and haunted.

"I'll wash yours," Kane told her innocently. He tipped his hat down low. "And I'll wash your front, too, ma'am —and anything else you've a mind to have tenderly touched."

She started to laugh a little breathlessly, and Kane felt a surge of dizziness. He groaned aloud. "Come on, my beloved bride. Let's get home."

She nodded, a little dazed. He gave her a boost up onto Cheyenne's back, mounted Thor, and proceeded to lead the race back to the ranch.

Joe Devlin really had a nice setup spread out for dinner. Chinese lanterns had been hung over the patio, candles were set all about, and two Mexican guitarists were playing light ballads and Spanish love songs.

It was a small party, but not exactly as small as Kane would have liked. There were a couple of neighboring ranchers in attendance, and Ed Rice—to Martine's obvious delight—had been picked up from the hospital for the night. Kane was touched to see her devotion to the man and a little humbled by her sheer pride in introducing the two of them.

It was the last of the senator's guests who gave Kane the shock he wasn't quite sure he managed to cover. And he was more than a little angry with Joe for not warning him ahead of time.

It wasn't until he and Martine were over by the bar,

sipping margaritas to a hail of congratulations, that Lisa made her appearance from the hallway. Joe seemed as disconcerted for a moment as Kane was surprised and annoyed. But then Joe seemed to gather himself together.

"Ah, Lisa, here you are. Uh, Kane, Martine, I'd like you to meet my goddaughter, Lisa Blank. Lisa, the newlyweds, Kane and Martine Montgomery."

At age eighteen Lisa had been a mischievous and frighteningly sensual young woman. Now, at twenty-three, she was really perfecting her craft.

She gave Kane a wickedly voluptuous smile and accepted his handshake regally, then grinned at Martine. "Hi. I've heard lots about you. It's a pleasure finally to meet you."

Kane noted that Martine returned the greeting politely. He also saw that she appeared a little confused, as if she had realized that Kane and Lisa already knew each other and weren't liking what was going on one bit.

Kane swallowed, trying not to wince visibly as a sharp pain seemed to tear at his gut. He wanted to wring Lisa's neck, then grab Martie and swear that what it appeared she was thinking wasn't true.

Except that he couldn't do it because he couldn't tell her the truth.

He moved closer to Martine and slipped an arm around her. He felt her stiffen, barely perceptibly, but she did stiffen. Kane silently cursed, only half aware of the conversations going on around them.

Joe himself seemed uncomfortable. Hell—they all were uncomfortable. And the more uncomfortable they appeared, the more he could sense that Martine was suspicious and angry.

"Let's eat, shall we?" Joe said at last.

Kane was glad in more ways than one when Ed Rice, his bad leg propped up on a second chair, picked up the conversation ball at the dinner table. Joe asked him how

124

in hell an old rancher like him had managed to get himself in such a predicament, and Ed seemed sheepish and dumbfounded for a moment before answering.

"Well, I tell you, it's still the damnedest thing, far's I can see. I was over by the cliffs, trying to round in a stray calf. All of a sudden out of nowhere comes a rock slide. Now I know dirt and rock falls from those little hills and crests all the time, but I also know that I've spent most of my life working the Four-Leaf Clover, and I ain't never seen anything like that before! My horse spooked, reared, and fell over backwards on me. And I was so spooked myself I let him fall on me." Ed shook his head with disgust and ran his fingers through the few wisps of hair that remained on the top of his head. "Must be gettin' old."

Martine set down her spoon in her fruit cup dish. "Old! Fiddle, Ed Rice!" she said with gruff emotion. "We're just incredibly lucky that you came out of this without being injured too badly. The Four-Leaf Clover just isn't right without you."

Ed laughed and looked down the table at Kane. "I hear tell the Four-Leaf Clover's doing great. I'm awfully glad you married that boy, Martine, else I'd be out of a job!"

The senator cleared his throat. Kane said smoothly that Ed would never have been out of a job. The fruit cups were cleared away, and Lisa very sweetly—too sweetly—asked both Martine and Kane questions about the Four-Leaf Clover.

It wasn't until they were settled in the living room after the neighbors had departed with all good wishes for the newlyweds that Joe narrowed his eyes and asked Ed another question.

"Ed, do you think anyone might have been up in those cliffs, maybe trying to spook your horse on purpose?"

Ed shrugged in the midst of rolling a cigarette. "I'd say

125

it was possible, Senator. But that's all I can say because I didn't see anything."

Kane leaned forward tensely. "But you do say it's possible."

Ed looked up at both men and then at Martine. She shrugged.

"A mystery! I love it!" Lisa exclaimed.

Kane glared at her. "Ed, it's important. You were hurt about the same time all the cattle were suddenly sick. And at the same time Martine was supposed to be paying back that loan."

"A loan she could have paid if so many of the cattle hadn't died off and others been ordered destroyed?" Ed asked.

"Yeah," Kane said.

Ed shrugged. "Sure, like I said, it's possible. But it isn't making a lot of sense. What would someone be doing in the cliffs if they were after the cattle? And why hurt me? My hide isn't worth anything on the open market."

"You're a damned good foreman—" Martie began defensively, but Joe Devlin interrupted her.

"Ed, Martie's right, you are a damned good foreman. But say you were someone trying to steal the Four-Leaf Clover out from under her. Look at the whole picture. She's got no savings to fall back on; they were depleted by medical bills. Knock off her cattle and her foreman, and she's in a hell of a bind. She can't pay a loan, and there goes her property. Ken Lander did it a few other times before he went for Martie."

Martine took a long sip of her cognac and stared at Joe, feeling a little ill and wishing they'd never come for dinner. She was already convinced that she was somehow, for some reason being lied to. Kane and Lisa knew each other. And now it appeared that there was more to her hard-luck ranch story than poor judgment and the will of God.

She didn't glance at Kane. She was feeling a little too uneasy to do so. Kane had spent a hell of a long time in the cliffs that morning. And he'd conveniently been there to apply for Ed's job.

"Joe, there's one thing you're forgetting. No cattle came down with diseases on those other ranches Ken Lander picked up. Do you really think he would go so far as to poison mine? And like Ed was saying, the cliffs wouldn't be the place to fool with the cattle. They're never over there. Ed was going after a stray. Otherwise he wouldn't have been there himself."

Martine started as she heard Kane inhale sharply. She gazed at him and found his eyes on her speculatively. Then it seemed as if an opaque mist had fallen over the green and gold glitter of his eyes. It was as if he had stiffened and closed himself off from her.

He stared across the table at Lisa, and Martine saw that she was now silent and a little pale. She was returning his stare.

What the hell was going on? Martine wondered, not sure if she was furious or ready to burst into tears.

"There's probably no connection," Kane said thoughtfully, "between the cattle and Ed's accident. Rocks do fall."

"That they do, young man," Ed said.

The senator, at Martine's left, patted her hand. "Martine, don't you worry about this any. I think Ken Lander was up to no good. I think he's been up to no good for a long time, but I'm on his tail, and you don't have to worry about it anymore. Give me half a chance, and I'll prove something against him!"

"Yes, but it was my ranch and my foreman. I've got to try to give you all the help—"

"It's our ranch," Kane said sharply, drawing her attention to him. His face appeared very hard again; his mouth was a white line against his bronzed features, set

127

and grim. "I'll deal with anything that has to do with Ken Lander. You stay away from him—and from any involvement in this whole thing."

His voice was so cool and curt that everyone went silent. Martine was stunned that he would speak to her so —especially in front of other people. She was tempted to dump her wine over his head—or burst into tears.

She swallowed carefully, determined not to make a scene, narrowing her eyes only to show Kane the depth of her anger. Then she rose with all the dignity she could muster. "Will you all excuse me, please? I feel the need for a little night air. And, Kane, if you don't mind, I'll worry about the ranch if I choose."

Martine felt as if her face were burning as she hurried from the living room to the patio. She walked straight to the rim of the pool and stood there, staring sightlessly at the water, glittering with the lantern candles' reflection. Eventually the breeze stirred to cool her heated flesh. She tried hard to think without letting her emotions cloud her view.

Kane . . .

He had been in such a hurry to marry. He had appeared at the ranch exactly when she needed him. Ed had broken his leg by the cliffs, right where Kane had spent the morning. And it didn't take that long to set a trap for a cougar, not nearly as long as Kane had been out there today.

She swallowed abruptly, trying to face facts. She had been attracted to Kane that first day, almost fatally attracted. She had been ready and eager to be touched by him, to make love with him, to fall in love with him, to lose her heart to him completely.

And she had married him—making the ranch as much his as her own.

Tears stung her eyes, and she fought them back. Ken Lander had been after her ranch and willing to take her as part of a bargain. Was Kane after the same thing—just more subtle and devious in his methods?

She pressed her hands to her face and discovered her fingers were shaking. She couldn't help remembering the afternoon. She had been so furious with him at the cliffs for jumping all over her. But he had touched her and cajoled her, and she had been back in his arms, laughing and breathless and as eager as he to reach the privacy of their bedroom and the intimacy of his caress once again—

"Hi. I thought you might like something to cool down with out here."

Martine spun around to see Lisa smiling at her, two frosted glasses in her hand. Lisa gave her a good-natured grin and offered one of the glasses.

Martie accepted it, studying the other woman. She was very attractive with full lips that could surely form a most alluring pout.

She knows Kane, Martie thought. Yet there was something about her that made Martine believe she was really interested in being friends.

"Thanks," Martine said, "what is it?"

"Margarita," Lisa said cheerfully, heading for one of the lounge chairs and propping her feet up. She assessed Martine carefully and laughed. "You were pretty cool in there. My hat's off to you." She chuckled softly. "He certainly can come off as the king of the castle, can't he? But really, I wouldn't be too upset. I mean, you do realize that it's all male bluster. He just wants to protect you —and I'd say he was jealous."

Martie grimaced and hoped she appeared casual as she took the lounge beside Lisa. "How well do you know Kane, Lisa?"

"What?" Startled, Lisa took a long sip of her drink, giving her attention to her straw. Then she smiled at Martine. "I don't know him at all. I just know men in

129

general, that's all. And your husband is kind of the hard and rugged type, you know. Independent, I'd say—and very possessive." Lisa grimaced. "They can be hard to live with, but you seem strong enough to hold your own!"

"Thanks," Martine said dryly. "Are you sure you don't know him?"

"Of course I'm sure!" Lisa laughed, and Martine wondered why she was lying.

"He's a grown man," Martine said bluntly. "I haven't known him long, but I've certainly never pretended to myself that he hasn't had any number of . . . relationships before he met me."

Lisa almost choked on her drink. Martine had to pat her back. Then she found Lisa's pretty—but watering—eyes on her.

"Martine, I assure you that I was never one of your husband's relationships!"

Martie frowned, lowering her head. Then why were they all lying? She wanted to scream, but she didn't. She smiled instead. They wanted to be subtle and play cat-and-mouse games; she could do the same. "Lisa, I was just wondering why we've never met. I've known Joe since I was a kid. And if you're his goddaughter . . ." She let the question trail.

Lisa grinned, apparently glad that the subject of their conversation had changed. "That's easy. I've never been here before. Joe always visits us. He and my dad are friends." She laughed. "I wonder if I should be insulted. He talks about you a lot, but I guess he never talks about me!"

Martine shrugged. "Well, it seems like it's been awhile since I've really talked to Joe anyway. Are your folks ranchers?"

"Yes," Lisa murmured, sipping her drink again. "And do I hate ranches!"

"Do you?" Her words were so bitter that they startled Martine.

"Yes!"

"You make it sound like a stigma."

"It is." She took a deep breath, then grinned. "Well, it seems to be to certain people who own vineyards anyway. Or maybe it isn't the ranch. . . . I'll find out soon enough."

Martie felt as if she were moving from one ridiculously confusing conversation to another. "What are you talking about?"

Lisa stared at her, then laughed ruefully. "Oh, nothing. I'm sorry." She hesitated, then grinned, and the bitterness in her voice was tempered when she spoke again with a touch of humor. "The usual boring story, I'm afraid. I fell rashly and foolishly in love with a man whose family decided I wasn't from the social sphere that I should be to be his wife. I'm getting over it. And it isn't the thing you're supposed to lay on a new acquaintance, is it?"

Martine shrugged. "Lisa, if he doesn't want you for a reason like that, then I think you're well rid of him."

"You're right, I'm not completely without confidence!" Lisa laughed, then stared at her drink again. "And I shouldn't love him, should I? Love is awful! We just don't seem to have any control over it, do we?"

"No, I guess we don't," Martine said softly. "But . . ." But what? Who was she to advise this woman when she had married a man she had come to realize she didn't trust?

"Ah, well . . ." Lisa hopped off her chaise lounge with the agility of a young gazelle. "I think I'm going to make myself another one of these things and go to bed. Martine, all the best to you and Kane. I know you're going to be a great couple, and it was really nice meeting you!"

"You, too, Lisa," Martine murmured. Lisa gave her a weak smile, then disappeared into the house.

The lantern candles were dying. It became very dark and gloomy on the patio, and all the luster of the night seemed to have disappeared.

With a sigh Martie decided that she would go in. Apparently Kane wasn't coming to her with an explanation or an apology. And eventually she had to drive home with him. It might as well be now.

But just as she started to rise she heard voices and footsteps coming from the living room out onto the patio. She didn't know why, but she froze.

Everything suddenly seemed to be shadows. Martine saw two men. Kane she knew from his height and his stance. Joe Devlin she knew from his voice—a gruff whisper now as he spoke.

"I don't like this one bit, Kane. I don't want to see her hurt. Why the hell did you have to marry her?"

A match flared in the dark; Kane lit a cigar and leisurely inhaled and exhaled before replying. "I married her for the same damn reason any man marries a woman, Joe. I love her. Don't you trust me?" His drawl had a slightly hostile tone to it. Because he was lying? Martine wondered, feeling sick. Or just because he was angry at the question?

She heard the senator sigh. "Kane, I know you, and dammit, yes, in most things I do trust you! But I know how important this other matter is to you. I just don't see why you had to rush into marriage. You were already sleeping with her!"

"That's nobody's business, not even yours, Joe," Kane said, a warning in his tone.

"Maybe not. Kane, you know how I feel about you. But I've got to watch out for Martie too. If you don't love her, don't ever let me find out about it. I respect you, son, and I care for you. I need your help right now too. But

132

hurt her in any way, and I'll blow everything you're doing sky-high, I swear it."

"Dammit, Joe!" Kane swore hoarsely. "I'm trying to keep her out of it all. I don't want her hurt again. I sure as hell don't want to ever catch Lander with his hands on her again. Joe, I'm telling you this because we're old friends, but so help me, I'll never explain or excuse myself again. I married her because I wanted her. Yes, I need to be on the Four-Leaf Clover, but the one doesn't have anything to do with the other. Good enough?"

"Good enough," Joe said quietly. In the darkness Martine could still sense him sizing up the other man.

She couldn't sense anything herself. She felt too numb to feel.

The tension between the two men suddenly seemed to dissipate.

"You didn't help things much, Joe."

"You mean Lisa?"

"You could have warned me."

"She just showed up. I didn't have time. But I—oh, brother! I forgot all about her. I'd better find out what she's up to."

The senator walked back into the living room. Kane paused for a minute, staring into the sky.

Martie forced her mouth to open. She was ready to jump up and confront him when he suddenly turned on his heel and returned to the living room.

Martine realized that she had grasped her fingers so tightly around the arms of the chair that they had cramped that way. She had to flex them forcibly to unwind them.

She was trembling as she stood but determined to have it out with all of them. They were lying to her. Why? If she confronted them, wouldn't they just deny everything?

She took a deep breath and decided that she would

133

make her own assaults on them, one by one, until she got to the bottom of things.

She stood on the dark patio awhile longer, breathing deeply to regain her composure. Then she went back into the living room. It was empty, but the front door was standing open, so she assumed that the others were out front.

She took one more deep breath and realized that she was still trembling inside. And why not? She had married a stranger. She had fallen in love with a man who was a mystery—and possibly a dangerous one.

"I will not fall to you again, Kane Montgomery!" she muttered with soft vehemence. And then she walked to the door and stepped outside.

Lisa was standing before Kane. His hands were on her shoulders. They had obviously just been exchanging some kind of intense words. Joe was nowhere to be seen.

"I'm going home," Martine said pointedly. Both Kane and Lisa jerked around, evidently startled by her appearance.

"Oh, well, good night again then," Lisa said, drawing cheerfully away from Kane. "Uncle Joe just took Ed back to the hospital. He won't be long, and I know he wasn't expecting you to return until he came back."

"Joe will understand, I'm sure," Martine said more icily than she intended. She looked at Kane, into the strange glitter of his hard eyes as he returned her gaze. "Kane can wait for Joe if he wishes."

She walked past both of them. Her vision seemed to be blurring, and she realized that she was very near to tears. She quickened her footsteps, hoping to leave Kane behind.

But from behind her she heard his long strides, then felt his fingers winding around her arm.

"Wait up!" he said harshly and, to her satisfaction, a little breathlessly.

She jerked her arm from his. "Stay here. I want to be alone."

"Why?"

"Because you're a liar and a fraud."

She reached the truck and jerked open the driver's door. But when she was seated, strong hands firmly propelled her across the vinyl to the passenger's side. She let out a number of furious epithets that made no difference. He was in the driver's seat, gunning the engine before she could move to hop back out of the vehicle.

"Kane, I do not want to be with you!" She spit the words out, trying to control her temper.

All she saw was shadows as they fell on the hard planes of his profile. He stared straight ahead at the driveway, grinding the truck's gears with a fury.

"You're my wife, Martine. And you are coming home with me." He spoke the words quietly but with a vehemence that left her trembling.

"Kane—"

The truck jerked to a halt. He turned to her, his arm stretching across the seat as he interrupted her.

"Lady, you swore a few vows to me. They may mean nothing to you, but they do to me. You don't want to be with me? Fine. But we will go home together. And I'll be damned if I sleep on any couch. If you want to discuss something rationally, I'll be glad to do so, but I'm going home first, and you're coming with me!"

She wanted to hit him and run from the truck. Not, she realized, that it would do her any good.

She clenched her fingers together in her lap and gritted her teeth.

The truck roared back into life, and Kane drove on silently.

Tears stung Martine's eyes again. She was shocked and confused and furious—and still in love with him, hating herself because she was.

"You bastard!" she yelled suddenly.

She didn't look his way but felt his chilling gaze fall briefly on her.

It was going to be a long drive home, she thought. Yet it turned out that the drive was not long enough at all.

It seemed only seconds later that they were at the Four-Leaf Clover. Then Kane was moving quickly. He was out his door and at hers before she could leave the truck. Taking her arm impatiently, he led her to the house.

"We are going to have this out!" she said defiantly.

His only reply was a bitter twist of his jaw.

CHAPTER SEVEN

Martine was relieved when he brought her to the kitchen. She realized that her teeth had been chattering, and she wondered with horror if she had really thought that he would drag her to the bedroom against her will. Could she actually have thought such a thing of a man she had married? The man she still loved—against all odds and reason?

He set her down at a chair before the table. She sat silently for a moment, vaguely aware that he was stalking about, making coffee.

"What are you doing?" she demanded at last.

"That's obvious, isn't it? I'm going to sober you up."

"What?" She was out of her chair in a flash; equally quickly he was back at her side, pressing her shoulders with tenderness to force her to sit again.

"If we're going to talk," he told her coldly, "I want you coherent."

"I am extremely coherent, Kane Montgomery! Nothing you say or do to throw blame on this other party is going to work! You knew Lisa before tonight. And you're up to something. You're not nearly as much in love with me as you are with this ranch. I want to know what's going on!"

He stared at her. His eyes seemed almost yellow as they narrowed. Silence fell. Then, as if from some distant world, Martine heard the steady beat of the coffee as it began to perk.

Kane placed his hands on his hips. "Why did you marry me?" he asked in a curious tone.

Martine lowered her eyes, certain she would choke on her answer. She could have never imagined that a single day could pitch her into such depths of misery after she had enjoyed a happiness so incredible and magical.

"You asked me to," she told him.

"Oh?" he said mockingly. "You would have married anyone who'd asked you?"

She stared at him, determined to be as cold as he—and not to cry. "I married you because I loved you."

"Loved?"

"Stop it, Kane!" Martine hissed, knotting her fingers in her lap. "I saw you with Lisa, and I heard you talking to Joe."

He was silent for a second. Then his fist slammed against the table. "Now you find it entertaining to eavesdrop on other people's conversations?"

"Eavesdrop?" she echoed heatedly. "I was on the patio when you two came out."

"I see. You just didn't think it would be important to make your presence known."

"I was too humiliated—having discovered my piteous self the center of the conversation," Martine said coolly. But the composed and cynical effect of her words was completely destroyed by the little sob that escaped her throat.

"Martine . . ."

His anger faded as quickly and completely as it had come. He was down on one knee before her, grasping her hands, reaching to touch her chin and draw her eyes to his.

"No, Kane, stop it!" she pleaded. "I want to know what's going on."

"I love you, Martine," he told her with quiet conviction, and her heart seemed to take a furious pound against her chest while flutters viciously attacked her stomach. It would be so easy to believe him. . . .

"It's not good enough, Kane," she said with a shaky swallow.

The pressure of his hand increased against her chin, forcing her eyes to meet his. "Martine, I asked you before why you married me. You said that you loved me. If you love me, I want you to trust me. I swear I love you. I married you because I do. And maybe I pressed you, maybe I was in a rush. Martine, the day I met you, you were under attack." He took a deep breath, and she was startled by the depth of feeling portrayed as he released it shakily. "I admit I've known some women, but Lisa isn't one of them. But because of all I've known in the past, I knew that you were unique, that I loved you, that I wanted you all my life. When I saw you that day, I wanted to be with you, to fight all your battles with you. There was fire about you—and vulnerability. I knew I wanted you. And once I had you, I knew that I wanted to love, honor, and cherish you all my life. Can't you believe that, Martine?" he asked wistfully.

She was silent for several seconds, very aware of the strength of his hands, tender now, aware of the power of his eyes, of his heat, his male scent. There was something disturbingly elemental about her feelings for him then. He was the man who could touch her and know her and make her feel so alive, so special. He could take everything from her, strip away her inhibitions, and give her mindless splendor. On a very base and shattering level, as old as time, she had become his, and perhaps he had become hers.

But these were not ancient times. Her heart, her emotions, and admittedly even her desires were swaying her mind. And no matter how much she loved and needed him, she could not allow herself to be a fool.

"I want to love you, Kane," she told him honestly. "I want to trust you. But I've been lied to. I can't trust you under those circumstances."

He stood then and turned his back on her, his hands on his hips. "Martine, I can't tell you exactly what's going on. I made a promise to someone else. A vow," he added, his tone becoming rueful for a moment, then becoming hard as he swung back to face her again. "If I swear to you that the matter has absolutely nothing to do with you and me, will you believe me?"

Martine decided that she did want coffee after all, just for something to do with her hands. She stood and poured herself a cup. "I—I don't know," she said at last, leaning against the counter and watching him as she sipped her coffee. "Maybe," she murmured a little breathlessly, "if you'll look at me and answer a few questions, I can try."

He raised a brow at her. "Shoot," he said a little coldly.

"What were you doing on the cliffs?"

"Trying to trap a cat."

"I don't believe you."

"Why not?"

She didn't answer that; she didn't really have any grounds to challenge him. "Were you up there the day that Ed had his accident?" she asked instead.

"What?"

"You heard me!" Martine retorted defensively. "Take a look at the whole picture, Kane." She continued quickly, afraid that she would lose her nerve as she sensed his temper, like heat from an oven, rising to fill the kitchen with tension. "Ed winds up in the hospital, so I need a foreman. Then you suddenly appear at my door, looking for a job."

He was silent for so long that she was tempted to throw down her cup and run from the kitchen. At last he muttered, "Bitch!" so softly that she wasn't even sure he'd spoken the word but rather had mouthed it. He took a step toward her, and she did set down her cup, vaguely hearing how it rattled as her fingers shook with the motion. She would have run then, except there was nowhere to go. His arms were like the bars of a cell as he planted his hands on the counter on either side of her, a tower of leashed rage as he spoke to her with crisply enunciated words.

"I can't believe that you would insult either of us so deeply with such a suggestion, but since you have, no, I did not cause Ed's accident. Nor would I ever do such a thing. I believe someone was on the cliffs that day, but it wasn't ME. Now, I'm going to tell you one last time that I love you. I've begged you to trust me. One day I can explain. I simply can't do it now. There's nothing I'm trying to take from you, Martine. You're just going to have to accept that."

She was almost afraid to speak, she had made him so furious. Yet she still couldn't believe that he would hurt her. If she believed that, then it would be all over. And she did love him, even if she was confused and miserable and angry.

"I—I can't accept it, Kane."

She closed her eyes and swallowed, alarmed at the sudden fire in his eyes. But then she felt him move away from her. She opened her eyes to see him striding from the kitchen. A second later the front door slammed.

Shaking, Martie sat down at the table and burst into tears.

There was no one to hear her as her ragged sobs filled the kitchen. It seemed that they went on and on. . . . She felt very, very lost and alone.

But at length she cried herself out. She forced herself

141

to rise and go to her bedroom, don a gown, and crawl into bed. She thought about locking the door against him. It would help prove her point.

But she didn't really want to prove any points. Whether it was foolish or not, she wanted to give him the trust he had asked her for. She wanted him to come home, to come to the bedroom, to shed his clothes and sleep beside her.

He did come back sometime during the night, or perhaps it was near dawn. By then Martie was so groggy that all she really knew was that he climbed in beside her, warm and strong and sleek.

But he didn't touch her; he lay on his side of the bed.

She was the one who could not bear the distance. With a sob she curled against him. Immediately his arms went around her. He pulled her close, and his words were a kiss, a caress against her forehead. "I love you, Martine. I love you so much it's part of me. I love you. . . ."

She nodded against his chest, just glad to have him beside her and terrified to break the moment with more words. She touched him as if she were afraid he wasn't real, her fingers trembling as she tentatively moved them over the muscles of his chest. She heard him suck in his breath and swallow hard; he was very still for a moment. Then he groaned, rolling to embrace her passionately, sliding his hand beneath her gown to caress her breast as he kissed her, his strong legs parting hers and coming between them. His hand roamed to that juncture, and in seconds she was gasping out inarticulate words as he stroked her intimately, finding the sweet source of her desire with the expertise of a lover who knew her well.

He was rough that night, very passionate and very demanding. He quickly brought her to a startling peak of pleasure, and before that could fully ebb, he was within her, strong and shattering as a storm, filling her as if he could indeed make them one.

142

Or perhaps leave his imprint on her like a brand forever. It didn't matter. She wanted him. She cherished the feel of him, the volatile climax, the sensation of drifting down in his arms, the sleek feel of his skin, the sensation of his weight on her. Holding him as they drifted to sleep, Martine prayed that it was right, that it was real.

A week later Martine sat in the office. She was supposedly working on the books, but not a single figure made sense to her, and she gave up all pretense of working to chew on the eraser at the end of her pencil.

She and Kane had spent the days in an uneasy truce. It was as if neither of them wanted to speak for fear of bringing on arguments or questions. In front of others they were unerringly polite and cordial.

Only at night, in the dark, were they really free to touch each other, when the words they spoke were whispered and husky and filled with hunger.

Martine exhaled a long, loud sigh. On Tuesday Kane had disappeared for the entire day. He had done so again on Thursday.

And now, Monday night, he was gone again.

He had given her no explanation for his absence, nor had she asked for one. She knew that if he would have given her an answer, he would have volunteered the information in the first place.

"I'm crazy!" she said aloud. "I must be."

Martine dropped the pencil and folded her arms over the desk to rest her head on top of them. How long could it go on? she asked herself miserably. She was not a weak woman, but she was acting like one. Did love make everyone weak? It shouldn't, she thought. It should make her strong and secure. . . .

Sighing, she raised her head with new determination. He had accused her of following him; she was going to start to do just that!

Having decided that she was going to be a snoop, she was going to do it all the way. He was denying her explanations for reasons of his own; she had to have explanations for reasons of her own.

A little uneasily Martine stood and looked down the hallway before locking the office door. Most of Kane's things were in her room now, but she had a hunch that anything he might not want her to find would still be in the office or in the foreman's room somewhere. She decided to go through all the drawers and files in the office first. Then she would attack the foreman's bedroom.

An hour later she had finished with the office and had been through everything in the foreman's room except for Kane's leather overnight bag. She hesitated briefly, feeling a little unethical and very squeamish about what she was doing. Then she reminded herself that she had married the man—a man who remained a stranger—and spent her nights sleeping with him.

If there was something dishonest going on, if the love was a lie, she had to know it.

She began to rifle through the bag: nothing but razor blades, shaving cream, shampoo, toothpaste, and a silver lighter. Sighing with frustration, Martine dropped the bag and sat cross-legged on the floor beside it, staring at it.

Then, slowly, she frowned. The bag looked deeper from the outside than it was on the inside.

She grabbed it again and by running her hands over the inner lining at last found a little tab. She pulled it, realizing that the bag had a false bottom. There she found a folded piece of paper in a plastic bag.

Shaking and swallowing and feeling her heart beat out like a wild drum, she picked up the plastic bag and very carefully pulled out the yellowing parchment within it. For long, long moments she stared at it in confusion, then realized that it was a map, one drawn up years ago.

144

It was a map of the Four-Leaf Clover.

She stared at it blankly for a long while, then somehow forced her mind to start working again. It was a treasure map of some kind. The marks on it led to the cliffs.

Fighting a wave of nausea, she strained her eyes against the almost illegible print. Eventually she was forced to admit the truth. It was very definitely a treasure map that led to a cache of gold—a cache of gold buried in the cliffs of the Four-Leaf Clover.

Martine started as she heard the front door open and slam. She had locked it, she knew. It could only be Kane.

She quickly returned Kane's things to his bag, except for the map. She put the bag back where it had been and sped to the office, where she secreted the map beneath a pile of vouchers. At the last second she thought to jump up and unlock the office door quietly. Then she sat back down, searching frantically for her pencil, and lowered her head over the books.

Just in time. The door opened, and Kane entered, frowning. His hat was angled over his eyes so that she could read nothing from his expression even as she prayed that hers was as unfathomable.

"You're still up working?" he asked.

"Yes," she said, hoping that the sound was louder than the thunder of her heart. "Where have you been?" she asked pointedly, determining that being on the offense was better than the defense.

"At Joe's," he said. "I had one of the cattle carcasses sent to a lab for analysis. They called today with the results."

"And?"

"It's possible they were purposely infected."

"Oh?" Martine stared down at her papers again. Dear God, she should care. But right now she couldn't believe anything. She suddenly thought that this whole thing was a ploy to divert suspicion from Kane.

"You don't sound as if you're even interested," he said slowly, accusingly.

She smiled at him with no warmth. "I'm not supposed to be, remember? You embarrassed me in front of a roomful of people to crack the whip and tell me so."

"Dammit, Martine," he said, cold anger rising in his voice. But then he shook his head with disgust. "I'm not going to argue with you."

"Good."

"I'm going to bed."

"Good night."

He hesitated for just a second. "You're not coming?"

"No. I'm not quite done here." Every muscle in her body seemed to knot with tension as she awaited his response. She felt as if he were poised like a tiger, ready to spring, and she almost screamed with the agony of the tension.

"Have it your own way." The door closed, not with a slam but quietly, resolutely.

Martine sat there trembling long after he had gone. Her mind went blank, then sped along, then went blank again. At last she managed to think coherently. The agony that seemed to pierce her heart had dissipated to a dull pain that shrouded her with a numbness she had to fight.

Kane believed there was a stash of gold on her property. She had always been able to convince herself that he loved her because he had put so much money into the ranch, but maybe he was just betting on much bigger stakes. . . .

A frightening thought knifed through her. It seemed very possible now that Kane had been on the cliffs the day of Ed's accident, looking for the gold. Perhaps he had caused the slide because Ed had almost discovered him.

She breathed deeply. Her heart was saying no. She

couldn't believe that she spent her nights making incredibly intimate love to a man who could be capable of attempted assault—or murder.

"It can't be!" she whispered aloud. And then: "What do I do?"

She had to do something.

She sat there for hours, staring into space. Finally she decided she would copy the map the next day and then demand some answers from Joe Devlin. Maybe, just maybe, she would get somewhere that way.

She jumped when the door suddenly opened. Kane, tall and angry—and totally unconscious of his nudity—stood there, glaring at her.

"It's almost four A.M. Will you please come to bed?"

"No," Martine murmured, lowering her eyes.

"Why not?"

She had to moisten her lips to speak. "I'm sorry, Kane. You can't tell me what's going on. I'm afraid that I—I don't want to sleep with you until you feel you can."

She stiffened at the furious sound of his expletive. And this time the door slammed with a thunderous reverberation.

Martine refused to allow herself to cry. Thankfully the numbness helped her now. At last she rose and returned to the foreman's room. She lay down on the bed, fully clothed, but she didn't sleep.

Kane was gone when she went out in the morning. Sonia was busy cleaning the house. She gazed at Martie with concern, but before she could say anything, Martine announced that she had to run into town.

She felt guilty for being so curt with Sonia, but she couldn't have been any other way. She was exhausted, and if Sonia had queried her, she might have given way to the tears she was so far managing to control.

As soon as she copied the map at the library, she hurried back to the Four-Leaf Clover and replaced the original in the false bottom of Kane's bag. Sonia, Martine noted with relief, was out back, adding chlorine to the pool.

Martine drove away quickly again, determined to talk to Joe. When she reached his place, the front door was standing open. Martie was about to call out his name when she happened to turn and see Thor tethered beneath the overhang of the barn.

Instinctively she entered the house in silence and walked quietly through the living room.

As she had somehow known she would, she saw Kane out on the patio. Joe wasn't there. Lisa was.

She and Kane were seated together on the lounges; Lisa was very intimately turned to him, touching his cheek.

"Kane, please! You've got to keep trying!"

"Dammit, Lisa, I am trying! I've made a nightmare out of my own life—"

"Oh, Kane!"

Lisa was no longer touching him; she had burst into tears. He stood but only to sit quickly by her side and take her tenderly into his arms. "Lisa, I think you're a little idiot, but I am trying, for you as well as Nan. Come on, Lisa, don't cry."

Martine never heard Lisa's reply. She backed out of the living room. She could have confronted the two of them, but she didn't want to. None of it mattered anymore; it was over. She was going to do two things by that afternoon: find the gold and contact her lawyer.

And she wasn't going to allow herself to dwell on the pain that seem to eclipse all else. The strangest thing about it was that nothing seemed to matter—except for the fact that he didn't really love her.

And no matter how horrible the situation, she still couldn't simply turn off the love she felt for him. But he never need know her feelings. Just because she was a fool didn't mean she had to act like one.

Yet this time she couldn't help the tears. She drove the truck through a mist of her own making to reach the cliffs. And then, before studying the map, she indulged herself in another torrent of sobs. When she sat back, exhausted from the draining effort and lack of sleep, she tried desperately to rise above her listless state by raging against Kane out loud—assaulting him with every curse she could think of.

Finally she began to study the map. Kane had already been looking for the gold, so it wasn't in an obvious place. Obvious! She started to laugh a little hysterically. Of course, it wasn't obvious! Who the hell ever buried treasure obviously?

She had to think. *Think*. She knew the ranch, she knew the cliffs better than anyone in the world.

For another thirty minutes, enveloped by the heat of the day yet heedless of it, she stared at the map. There was a star at the place where the "treasure" was supposed to be. A star, a star, a star . . .

She stared up at the cliffs, perversely glad of the puzzle that was taking her mind somewhat off her own misery. And then, just like a flash of light, she understood.

The star was where five boulders encircled one of the strange cave formations. Shaking with nerves and excitement, Martine slammed out of the truck and hurried up the rock-strewn path, a shovel tossed over her shoulder and a flashlight in her pocket.

It took another half hour of uphill walking to reach the place, and then she spent an hour digging in absolute frustration. She almost upset a sleeping rattler and then panicked and ran out. But it was probably a good and sobering thing, she decided. Her close brush with the venomous fangs had taught her quickly that she was fond

149

of living and that she needed to take care with what she was doing.

She didn't touch any rocks or stones again with her bare hands but cautiously used the shovel for even the smallest movement. She was about to give up, certain that the map was a fake and that no gold really existed, when she lifted a rock at the far left of the cave, slammed the shovel down hard with exasperation—and heard a metallic clink. With renewed excitement she began to dig again, and this time her efforts were rewarded.

The box she dug up was about a foot high and deep and three feet long. There was a lock on it, one that frustrated her almost as much as the search. By the time she swung the shovel for at least the fifteenth heave, she fell with its downward motion, gasping for breath and drenched with rivulets of sweat.

But that final heave had broken the lock. She cautiously used the shovel to open the box—and was bedazzled as it fell open and the glare of her flashlight picked up an almost ethereal golden glow.

The box was filled with nuggets—raw nuggets of gold. Martine had never been more stunned in her life—or more bitter. All the time when she had so desperately been trying to make a go of it, there had been a fortune awaiting her on her own property.

And she had been so touched by Kane's determination to put his own money into the ranch! She didn't know much about gold, but she did know that there were pounds of it here—even in this raw state. The box had to be worth a small fortune.

"Oh, God!" she cried, shaking as she sat in the dirt.

She just kept staring at the gold, telling herself over and over again that Kane had married her because of it. Yet no matter how foolish it was, she just couldn't really force herself to believe it could be true.

She should go to the police, she knew. But she didn't

want to—not yet. She could go to Joe Devlin and present him with all the evidence and demand an answer. Surely Joe would never have sent Kane to her if he were nothing but a fortune hunter!

Martine suddenly forced herself to get up. It was going to take her twice as long to get back to the truck as it had taken to get here; she was going to have to drag the gold with her.

It didn't take her twice as long; it took her four times as long. Her back was in agony from the effort, her palms were scratched and bleeding, and she was as soaked as she might have been had she plunged headfirst into water.

But she made it. And straining and grunting and panting, she managed to get the box into the small trunk compartment built into the back of the truck.

She glanced at the sun. It was starting to fall, but she probably had time to hurry back to the ranch and shower and leave before she would have to face Kane again.

But she had pressed her luck too far. She was standing in the shower, thinking that it was probably dangerous to have a fortune in gold in a truck sitting in her driveway, when her breath seemed to stop completely.

The door to the bathroom had opened, and the shower curtain had been ripped back.

Kane, his arms crossed comfortably over his chest as he leaned against the sink, was staring at her with no apology whatsoever for invading her privacy.

She was so stunned to see him that at first she couldn't react. But then she did, wrenching at the curtain and screaming out something about his having no right.

The curtain was wrenched open again. "I have a lot of rights," he reminded her coolly, "even if you've chosen to deny a few of them."

Shaking, Martine turned off the water and groped for a towel. Kane handed her one. She quickly mopped the water from her face and struggled to cover herself. His laughter unnerved her.

"I know every inch of your flesh better than you do yourself, Mrs. Montgomery," he said coolly. "What you think you're hiding, I don't know."

Martine dropped the towel and hurried out of the bathroom to start opening her drawers, suddenly at a complete loss to find her clothes.

Kane came up behind her. His hands were very dark as they encircled her waist, his fingers splaying over her hips and abdomen. Martine went still. She was so tired that she could barely think, so unnerved by his touch that she could barely remember the horrible things she knew to be true. More than anything, she wished she could fall back against his chest, let him touch her and love her and then lull her to sleep.

"Kane, let go of me. Please." There was a tremor of beseeching in her voice that was very earnest. She lowered her head, afraid that she was close to being broken. "Please, Kane?" she whispered, and her whisper shook. "I told you that I—I just couldn't trust you anymore."

His hand moved upward, over her breast, his thumb grazing her nipple, his palm caressing the fullness of the mound's weight. Martine closed her eyes and clenched her teeth, reminding herself that it was all a lie.

"Martine . . ." Her name was the closest thing she had ever heard to a plea from him.

A lie, all a lie.

She shoved away from him and at last found the right drawer for panties and a bra, which she awkwardly, blindly fumbled into. "What do you want?" she asked harshly.

"I want to slap you across your backside and suggest you grow up before you completely destroy a good marriage," he said harshly.

Martine shivered. "When you're ready to talk to me," she said smoothly, "I'll be ready to listen."

"Oh, I'm ready to talk. You took off with the truck today without telling a soul. I needed it."

She laughed bitterly. "It's my vehicle, Kane. I don't have to tell anyone when I wish to use it. In fact, I'm using it again tonight."

"Oh? Where are you going?"

"Out."

Trying to remain very composed and determined, she turned to walk across the room to the closet. But she hesitated when she caught his eyes on her. They were narrowed slits, gleaming as brilliantly as the gold in the box—

"Out where?"

"What the hell difference does it make?" she inquired with a ragged snap.

Very slowly, so slowly that she was beguiled to immobility, he began to walk toward her. At that moment she wasn't sure if she was too terrified to move or still so fascinated and in love that she was too stupid to be terrified.

He stopped right before her. His fingers threaded into the hair at the nape of her neck; they caressed her, yet they were firm in a way that brooked no opposition.

"It makes all the difference in the world," he told her harshly. "You're my wife. . . ."

The word lingered on his lips as he lowered them to hers. "I love you."

The words were formed against her mouth before he kissed her: a kiss that was deep and tender and coercive and firm and consuming, robbing her of all strength. She was very, very tired.

She was too exhausted to fight him, too vulnerable, too determined not to believe the evidence that she had discovered herself.

A small sob of protest escaped her, and that was all. He lifted her into his arms and laid her on the bed. She watched him almost distantly as he began to strip off his shirt.

"You're having an affair with Lisa," she told him. "I don't want you touching me."

"What?" he demanded as his jeans joined his shirt on the floor.

"I saw you together."

"You didn't see us 'together.' I admit that I know Lisa, but I swore to you that I'd never had an affair with her."

He lay down beside her, staring into her eyes. How could he be lying? she wondered.

He pressed his lips against her collarbone. His fingers found the clasp to her bra and released it, and he rested his head against her breasts, touching them with the greatest tenderness.

"I swear to you, I'm not having—nor have I ever had —an affair with Lisa."

"Why do you keep lying to me?" she whispered.

"I don't lie to you," he said.

She closed her eyes and kept them closed as he made love to her. She could not deny the sensation, the magic of his touch. She wanted desperately to believe in him. . . .

He made love to her slowly, tenderly, drawing out the eroticism, bringing her to a frantic need.

And when it was over, he began again.

He didn't leave her until she was drifting into an exhausted slumber. Only at that point did she start to wonder—in a mind already lost to dreams—if he hadn't loved her so passionately and thoroughly because he knew full well that she would then sleep and stay in for the night.

Out of commission, as it were.

154

To give him more time?

Time for what?

Sleep claimed her. There could be no answer to the questions. Not that night.

CHAPTER EIGHT

Martine didn't expect to find Kane next to her when the sun woke her in the morning. She didn't.

But she was surprised to find a note on his pillow. "Please believe in me," it read. "I love you."

She smiled slightly and closed her eyes, trying to decide if she was an idiot, completely daft or—or if her instincts were right. Kane did love her, and he would talk to her as soon as he could.

She groaned aloud. How could she be right when her truck was parked out front with a fortune in it that she had never known existed before she had discovered Kane's map? How could she be right when she had actually seen him holding Lisa, promising that he would do something for her, soothing her tears?

The phone started ringing then. Martine cast her arm over her eyes, assuming that Sonia would be in the house and would answer it. Apparently Sonia wasn't in the house, for the phone kept ringing. Martine fumbled a hand over the nightstand until she found the extension to answer the shrilling summons.

"Hello?"

There was silence for a moment and then a man's voice —a voice that could still send chills of distaste to her stomach to bind it in knots.

"It's Ken Lander, Martine. Mrs. Montgomery, that is," he said caustically.

She didn't say anything. "Don't hang up on me, Martine!" he said quickly, obviously having a certain amount of ESP since that was exactly what she had been about to do.

"You see, Martine, I can tell you a few things you probably want to know by now about that Mr. Western Macho you decided to marry."

"There's nothing you could say that I'd want to hear," Martine replied. But she couldn't keep a certain hesitance out of her voice. Ken did sound as if he knew something. And at this point she had such a nagging sense of desperation to get at the truth. . . . But not from a man who has almost raped her!

"Ah, so all is not ecstasy in paradise, eh?" Ken said slyly. "Want to meet me somewhere?"

"No," she said with more conviction. "I know everything about Kane that I need to know," she said sweetly. "I love him. That's good enough for me. Good-bye."

"Where is he right now, Martine? Do you know that? I'll bet you don't. But if you've a mind to find out, try the old wooden house on Grayfeather Road."

She didn't get a chance to hang up on Ken. He hung up on her.

In lieu of having Ken to hear her, Martine told the phone a few things about him. Then she crawled out of bed, showered, and decided she wouldn't get anywhere with her thoughts until she had a cup of coffee and something to eat. She'd slept through dinner the night before and crawled through the caves instead of having lunch.

Coffee was easy enough. Someone had already made it and left it on the stove. She tried to cook a few eggs and discovered she was so distracted she burned them.

Heating up the chili seemed her best bet even if chili didn't tend to find a place on many breakfast menus.

By the time she had eaten and pondered through a second cup of coffee, a spasm of panic hit her. If Ken was

right and Kane was out on Grayfeather Road somewhere, he had probably taken the truck—the truck that
was her hiding place for the gold.

She leaped up from the table and raced to the window,
knocking her chair over and almost ripping the curtain
from its rod. Then she heaved a sigh of relief so great that
it made her dizzy. The truck was still in the drive.

But after in vast relief she had leaned against the sink
for a moment, she frowned and turned back to the window.

The truck was in the drive, and Thor was in the left
pasture, rolling around in the dirt at the moment and
making a dusty mess of himself. Cheyenne was out there
too. In fact, between the left and right pastures, she could
account for all the horses except three; the geldings always used by Sonia, Bill, and Jim when they were moving
the herd.

She gnawed nervously on her thumbnail for a moment,
then threw her hands into the air. There was no help for
it. She knew damned well she was going to take a drive
down Grayfeather Road.

Seconds later she was in the truck. "I know I'm crazy
now!" she told herself aloud. "Driving down dirt roads
with a fortune of gold stuck in an old truck."

But crazy or not, she was doing it.

Grayfeather Road was about five miles from her ranch,
fronting property that was reservation land belonging to
the Apache. Martine knew the Indians' land fairly well;
she had grown up and gone to school with many her own
age, made a number of fairly good friends, and did business with them now. Almost everyone in hard cattle land
like this did business together. Whites and Indians alike
were clannish around here; their land was the common
factor.

But she couldn't remember an old wooden house out
on Grayfeather. When she turned the corner onto the

road, she pulled off onto the embankment for a moment and narrowed her eyes to try to recall. At last she let out a little cry of triumph, certain that the house was behind a small scattering of tall pines.

She drove slowly until she reached the pines, then pulled the truck off the road and into their shelter. She could see the house. It was an old Victorian structure, set up on a sloping hill. Martine got out of the truck and started gnawing at her thumbnail again.

There was a snazzy little Ferrari parked in front of the house, and Martine had seen the car before. She knew she had. Ferraris were hard to miss in these parts.

The Ferrari had been parked at Joe Devlin's the night they had gone for dinner. It had to be Lisa's.

Then, even as she stared up at the house, she inhaled sharply and stepped back into the trees. The front door opened, and Kane and Lisa stepped out.

Lisa appeared upset; Kane threw his arms up in the air, stared at the sky, and murmured something. Then he pulled his hat down over his forehead and slipped a comforting arm around her shoulder and led her slowly to the Ferrari.

Martine watched them, slinking as far back into the trees as she could. Kane was driving, and he must have been in a frustrated mood. The Ferrari sped down the drive and onto the road.

Martine felt plunged into confusion and misery once again. Oh, God, how she wanted to trust Kane! And just this morning—despite the damning evidence of the map and the gold—she had convinced herself that she did.

And now . . .

She felt sick and dizzy. She planted her hands on the knees of her worn jeans for a moment and bent over for strength. Then she straightened and started walking up to the old wooden house on the hill.

It wasn't a long walk. Soon she was climbing the two

159

steps to the porch and walking across the weathered wood. The front door was slightly ajar. She swallowed a little nervously and peered inside. It seemed very dark inside, muted and musty. The furniture was as period as the house. There was an old piano, well polished and gleaming even in the darkness. Wing-back overstuffed chairs sat before a fireplace, and an old sofa was in the center of the room.

"Can I help you, miss?"

The words were softly, laboriously spoken in a cracked and husky voice. Martine started, realizing that in the dimness she hadn't seen the old woman sitting in a rocker in the far corner of the room.

Very nervously—and more than a little shamefully—she stepped into the entryway. "I didn't mean to pry," she said apologetically, and then paused. Blinking against the shadows of the house, she saw that the woman was very old. She looked to be near a hundred, with bronzed skin, creased and leathered by the years. But her hair was still very dark, with no touch of gray to it. It was long and braided into two plaits. So dark . . . As dark as the eyes that looked into hers, ancient with their sadness yet somehow wise. She was Apache, Martine knew. And Martine thought the woman carried all the dignity and pride and beauty of her tribe within those dark, haunting eyes.

"You may come in," the woman said.

"Thank you—" Martine began.

But she never finished. She issued a little scream as a hand fell on her shoulder, the fingers tightening like steel vises. She didn't need to turn then to know it was Kane; she knew his subtle masculine scent, and she knew the tense feel of his body behind hers.

"She doesn't need to come in, Nan. This is Martine, my wife, who seems to have a real problem with minding

160

other people's business," he said, his voice taut with controlled fury and displeasure.

"Kane." The old woman protested, lifting a hand.

"Nan, I'm very, very sorry. I'll get her out of here now," he said gruffly.

And he meant it. He shoved Martine around and prodded her firmly out the door, then closed it sharply behind him. She stared at him, trying to find the lover she had known during the night.

That man was gone. She didn't know this Kane. His face was as dark and tense as a stormy sky. His eyes met hers with a merciless blaze.

"Nothing ever means anything to you, does it, Martine? You just have to stick your nose everywhere and you don't care who you hurt. Well, I'm sorry, this is one time when I don't give a damn what you think about me." His lips were compressed tightly as he grabbed her arm and dragged her forcefully from the porch. Panicked and furious, Martine tried to break his hold but she couldn't.

"Dammit, let go of me, Kane!" She lashed out at him. How in hell had he gotten back there? she wondered. The red Ferrari was gone. "Kane, let go of me! If you don't want me to care about what's going on, that's fine. I won't dream of coming near you again. But so help me, you'll get out of my house and off my ranch!"

His expression didn't alter one bit, but then it was like stone, and stone didn't soften or change. He just kept walking, dragging her so that she tripped to keep up. "Surprised to see me, Martine, you sneaking, conniving little bitch! You should have hidden the truck, then I wouldn't have known you were here. You're a hell of a spy." He grated out the words, as if he hadn't heard her at all. "I'll be damned if I do understand why you married me! Unless it *was* to spend your days playing spy!"

They had reached the truck, but his grip was still like

steel, his face like the furious clouds of a storm. Martine didn't care.

"Me? You are the most arrogant bastard I've ever met in my life. Lying, cheating, conniving! How dare you question me? You married me for the gold. For the *gold!*"

At least she'd caught his attention. But she wasn't glad that she had. She suddenly found herself with her back pressed to the truck, his arms imprisoning her there. "What do you know about the gold?" he demanded.

She fought hard to raise her chin, narrow her eyes, and spit out her answer with contempt. "I found your map."

He laughed dryly and bitterly. "Ah, yes. Ms. Spy. I should have known you would have torn everything apart until you found it."

"Well, I'll tell you what, Mr. Montgomery." She tried to speak coolly. "You've got one more day to find the gold for you and your precious Lisa. Today. I don't give a damn about it. You can bring out a whole search party while I ride into town. Nothing behind your back, Kane. Not like the treatment I receive. I'm telling you flat out that I'm filing for a divorce and I want you out of the house by tonight."

He moved away from her. "Get into the truck."

"I will not," she replied, realizing that he meant to get in with her.

"Yes, you will," he said curtly. "Where are the keys?" She stood stubbornly mute, desperately wondering if she had pushed him too far, if he was more ruthless than she had ever been willing to believe.

He smiled slightly. "Give me the keys, Martine. Unless, of course, you prefer me to find them myself. I will, you know."

She hesitated for a moment, both defiant and frightened. But she knew that he meant what he was saying, and she certainly didn't want the indignity of a search.

"Why?"

"You've got two seconds to hand them over, Martine."

She reached into her pocket and handed him the keys. "Get in," he repeated.

"No."

She found herself hoisted into the truck. Seconds later he was speeding along the road.

"Kane, you're going to have to let me out of this truck sometime," she drawled at last with all the cool disdain she could muster. *"Kane!* Just let me out! You can go search for your stinking gold. . . ." Her voice trailed away as she remembered that the "stinking gold" was in the truck.

He turned, flashing her a smile with no humor or warmth. "I am going to go search for the gold. So are you."

"What?"

His eyes returned to the road. "You're so determined to know what's going on, I'm going to let you find out. But you see, I can't—not unless I can find the gold. So we'll go together."

Martine swallowed nervously. "I told you, I don't care what's going on. I just want out of it."

"You're my wife," he said softly.

"No, never really!" She said challengingly. "All you wanted was the ranch. Well, according to the law, my property is yours. You've got your rights."

He smiled again, interrupting her. "Rights, huh? There are only very certain and specific rights I ever wanted from you, Martine: those usually given freely with love, tenderness, devotion—and trust. Well, I don't suppose I can beat the fact that I love you into you. And right now I'm so mad I'm not sure I care. But, beloved spouse, you are going to spend some time with me treasure hunting. Anyone who has snooped around with such dogged determination as yours deserves to be in for the finale."

"I'm not going with you!" Martine yelled.

He smiled again—the hard smile that chilled her to the bone. "You're coming with me."

She held her silence for a moment, certain by his course that he meant to go by the ranch house first. With any luck someone would be around to save her.

But no one was. Kane made sure that no one would be around later, either, by writing out a note that explained they were going to camp out for a few days.

And he didn't let her go for an instant. He was in a rare, rare temper. His anger was controlled—not once did he hurt her—but not once did he let her go as he moved through the house, collecting clothing, blankets, water, and foodstuffs.

Only when he was forced to relinquish his hold to load the truck did he do so. Martine stared mutely at him for a moment, then turned in a sudden whirl and raced back to the house.

He caught her on the porch. Again he didn't hurt her. He just held her and smiled politely. "Mrs. Montgomery, you can set your rear into the truck or I can do it for you. The choice is yours."

She squared her shoulders, stiffened her spine—and walked to the truck. She didn't doubt him for a moment. Not in his present mood.

The long drive to the cliffs was made in total silence. Kane pulled the truck higher up the ridge than she had. He knew exactly where he wanted it: near the star.

"We'll sleep in the cave," he said curtly.

"What about snakes?"

He raised a brow to her. "Have you seen snakes up here?"

"Rattlers. They're always around the rocks."

"We'll just make sure we've got clear space and that we aren't disturbing any nests. Come on, let's unload."

"You're crazy if you think I'm going to help you do anything," Martine said, not moving.

164

He shrugged and got out to do it himself.

After pulling out the blankets, food, and clothing, he paused, leaning against the driver's window to stare at her across the seat. "Is the torch still in the trunk bin?" he asked.

Yes, but so was the gold!

She lowered her lashes to hide her growing panic. "I'll get it!" she said quickly.

"I thought you weren't going to help?"

"Just leave me alone and I'll get the damn flashlight."

He shrugged. Martine got out of the truck, waited for him to retreat to the cliff, and then got the flashlight, her heart beating furiously as she saw that the gold box was still there.

What would happen if he spent days digging only to discover that she had had it all along? If she could just get the keys to the truck away from him, it wouldn't matter.

But when the sun set that night, she began to wonder uneasily if it would matter. She had spent the day sitting stonily in the shade of the cliff; Kane had spent the day splitting rock and digging. Bare-chested, he had spent hours swinging pick and shovel, and she had been left to watch the muscles play beneath the bronze tan of his glistening flesh.

And to wonder dully why she still wanted desperately to believe that it all was a nightmare, that some miracle would explain his behavior, that she could love him again.

He made their dinner, and she was too hungry to refuse the stew he cooked over an open fire.

Ironically he had brought wine. In her misery Martine decided she might as well drink it.

After they had eaten and Kane had set the plates aside, he sat across the open fire from her, still bare-chested,

165

watching her as he poured out the last of the bottle of wine between them.

"Are you planning on killing me?" she asked bluntly.

"Killing you?" He was incredulous.

"This is kidnapping, you know."

"In a sense, I suppose it is," he replied. "But then," he added lightly, raising his glass in the air, "we could think of it romantically, you know. Newlyweds beneath the stars."

"If you touch me. I'll scream my head off."

Kane laughed again. It seemed that his temper had faded at last; he had beaten it out on the rock. "Martine, I'm willing to bet that if you believed in the least some-one could hear you, you'd have been screaming long before now. But don't worry, I've no intention of touching you."

Martine blinked, wondering if he meant it.

"Who's the old Indian woman?" she asked.

"A friend," he said curtly.

"What is the relationship between you, Lisa, and her?"

"None of your business—unless I find the gold."

He rose then and stretched. "Will you excuse me if I prove to be less than entertaining tonight, darling?" he drawled. "I'm really bushed."

To Martine's absolute amazement he prodded the fire to a satisfactory blaze, grabbed a blanket, and curled up beneath the shale.

She wished it could be so easy for her.

And then she was glad that it wasn't. She waited for a long while until she heard his deep, even breathing.

She rose as quietly as she could, found his discarded shirt and denim jacket, and very methodically went through the pockets. To her frustration, the keys to the truck weren't in any of them. With an oath of disgust she threw his shirt back to the ground, only to be rewarded by his husky chuckle.

166

"Sorry, sweetheart. They're in the pants."

Was there a slight innuendo to his words? At the moment she was too angry to care. She found her own blanket and curled up for a very miserable night.

By the morning she was stiff and sore and truly irritable. She wasn't sure if she cared whether or not he had thoughts of doing away with her. Of course, that was probably because she didn't believe—couldn't believe—that he would hurt her.

Kane had breakfast ready. Bacon and eggs and hard rolls, all well prepared. But then she didn't doubt that he had been around ranches all his life, and ranchers tended to know how to survive in the open.

She ate in rigid silence and was surprised when he told her he intended to drive to the stream for water and to wash.

He smiled at her suddenly eager expression.

"Don't raise any false hopes, Martine. Sonia will be at the ranch house today, and Bill and Jim will be branding calves."

"How do you know that?"

"I run a tight ship," he said briefly.

They were alone at the stream, completely alone. Without a glance her way, Kane stripped and plunged in, obviously enjoying the clean water against his flesh. "Aren't you coming in?" he asked cordially.

She felt sticky and dusty and miserable and longed to dive in. But she was also horrified by the thought that although she believed his promise that he wouldn't touch her, she didn't trust herself. It still hurt too badly. She had fallen too deeply in love to fall out of it easily; she had become too accustomed to his body joining with hers. . . .

"I don't trust you," she said sweetly.

"I told you I won't touch you."

She shrugged, then realized his pants were on the embankment. She tried to wait until he seemed unaware of her, still standing there. Then she hurried down to grab the pants quickly and rifle through the pockets.

It was no good. She had barely touched the jeans before he rose from the water in front of her and she found herself fully dressed and soaking in the stream.

"Martine," he told her very softly, "you're not leaving. We're in this together now, you and I."

"I hate you," she told him.

He gave her a crooked, pained smile that almost managed to brush her heart. "Why couldn't you ever just trust me?" he asked with a whispered agony that seemed to pull and tug at her soul and make her wish desperately all over again that there was some reason in it all.

She turned her back on him and swam a little down the stream. Moments later he stood on the bank, dressed in jeans again. "Take off your wet things. I'll bring you dry clothing."

The clothes were on the shore, and Kane was nowhere to be seen. Miserably Martine shed her soaked things, splashed in the fresh water again, and dressed.

Kane was waiting for her in the truck.

The rest of the day was similar to the one before it. Martine sat rigidly; Kane plowed away at rock and earth.

That night they ate hot dogs and drank burgundy.

"What happens if you don't find the gold?" Martine asked.

The firelight was reflected in his eyes. "I'll find it." He smiled at her devilishly. "I've got lots and lots of time. And lots of faith."

"What if the map is a sham?"

"It isn't. I know a friend of the man who buried the gold."

Martine stared at him hesitantly for a moment. "Kane, were you here the day that Ed was hurt?"

"No, I wasn't," he said flatly. Then he rose again and fixed the fire. "Good night, Martine."

He got his blanket and curled up by the rock wall. Martine gazed into the fire, bleakly realizing this could go on interminably. She desperately needed to get away from him, but she could never make it on foot. She had to have the keys.

In frustration she curled up a little outside the cave entrance, staring up at the stars. Hours passed and a coyote began to howl in the distance. Martine shivered, remembering that they had never caught the prowling cougar. A wildcat wouldn't bother her—she knew that—not unless she bothered it. But she was suddenly frightened and longed to curl up beside the man who had surely kept to one promise, the one he had made not to touch her.

The keys, she reminded herself, were in his pants, if she could only get his pants off. . . .

And then she was ashamed of herself for thinking of seducing a man—even if he was legally her husband—when she suspected there was something untrustworthy about him.

But as the coyote continued to howl she reminded herself that she had already made love with him dozens and dozens of times.

And somewhere in the middle of the night she stood, shed her clothing, and walked over to him.

"Kane!" she whispered.

He opened his eyes, astonished. She stood over him, tall and sleek, yet as beautifully curved and luscious as a nymph come to torment his dreams. He desperately wanted to reach out and touch her, to smooth back the auburn hair curling around the firelit silk of her flesh.

Instead, he smiled bitterly. "You're not getting the keys, Martine."

She spit out an oath and flounced back to her own

169

position, sitting before the fire, her knees drawn up, her arms crossed and rested over them. Wearily she closed her eyes and put her head on her arms.

She was so angry, he thought bitterly, that she didn't even realize she was still naked.

He rose and went over to her. He hunched down on the balls of his feet beside her to reach tenderly for her chin. She didn't fight him. She just stared at him with such misery that he wanted to forget the whole thing.

But he couldn't, not now. If he didn't find the damned gold, he'd never be able to really clear himself in Martine's eyes.

"Nan, the Indian woman, is very dear to me, Martine. I made a promise to her that I would never mention her name to anyone unless I did find the gold. When she was young, she was very deeply hurt. She sees few people. I would have brought you there eventually."

"But you did bring Lisa," Martine said, hurt and bewildered.

He hesitated for a long while. "Lisa is her granddaughter." Once again, he paused. "And my cousin."

"Cousin!" Martie gasped. "Why didn't you just tell me that in the first place?"

"When I find the gold, I'll explain the whole thing. I swear." He smiled painfully at her, dared brush her forehead with a kiss, then returned to his own place against the rock.

For a long while he lay there with his heart beating like a drum, praying breathlessly, clenching his jaws together so tightly they hurt.

And then his prayer was answered. "Kane?"

He spread open his blanket. She lay down beside him, and he shook when he touched her.

"Kane, I have to tell you something," she whispered.

"Not tonight," he told her raggedly. "Not tonight, please. Love me, Martine. Trust me . . . if just for tonight. Be my wife and my lover. Hold me. God, but I missed touching you. . . ."

He did so then, reverently. The dirt floor became a bed of soft clouds for them both. Never had making love been more beautiful, for each touch was stressed by words of love and assurance, words that overlapped one another, mattering tremendously and not mattering at all. . . .

"I still don't understand, but it doesn't matter—"

"I kept losing my temper because I was so afraid I was going to lose you—"

"I couldn't stop loving you. Even now I have to trust you because I can't stop—"

"I had to keep my word, you'll understand—"

"Dear God, I think I'd die without you—"

"Oh, Martine, touch me, hold me—"

"Kane—"

Nothing was really explained. It really didn't matter. Through it all Martine felt bliss and contentment and splendor.

She had never been foolish—only when she doubted him. Her love had always been the truth; she was fully convinced of that now.

And in the morning she would point him to the gold, and they would laugh. . . .

And then his mystery would be explained. Right now it didn't matter. No gold on earth could compare to that of his eyes when he was warmed and brightened by his desire, his tenderness, the love she fully believed in. Nestled in his arms, she was convinced that the cave was the most beautiful, romantic place on earth. So, content with the present and the thought of the future, she slept.

Martine awoke knowing something was wrong, yet confused about what it was.

The fire was burning. She could smell coffee perking.

With her eyes still closed, she knew that the coffee was almost ready—

That was what was wrong. Coffee shouldn't have been ready, because Kane was still beside her. She could feel his body beside her own.

She opened her eyes and gasped. She was staring down the long nose of a double-barreled shotgun.

"Good morning, Mrs. Montgomery," Ken Lander said cordially, not moving the shotgun from her face. He smiled, and she thought again that it was such a pity such an attractive smile could hold such venom. She swallowed, drawing the blanket around her nudity, wondering why Kane didn't wake.

"What do you want?" She glanced quickly at Kane's shoulders; he didn't move.

Ken Lander laughed; the sound was absurdly good-natured. "He's not going to wake up, Martine."

"What do you mean?" she exclaimed, wanting to touch Kane yet terrified to do so.

"Oh, he's not dead—yet," Lander said. "They say the strongest man has his weakness. You were Kane's, Martine. You see, I came in here while you were still sleeping like a baby. I told him I'd slit your throat if he came too near me, and when I asked him, the man turned around as docile as a lamb. Went down like a damned mountain lion, though. But he should be out of it for a while, at least long enough for me to talk to you."

"Talk about what?" she demanded hoarsely.

"The gold, Martine."

"I don't know what you're talking about."

"You always could lie with your nose in the air, Martine."

"All right. I know about the gold. We were digging, the same as you were." She took a deep breath. "If you get off my property now, you haven't committed any crime. If you keep that gun pointed in my face too long—"

"Oh, but I have committed a crime, and Lover Boy there has just about enough on me to prove it. Martine, you must be the only woman alive courageous enough—or stupid enough—to argue with a shotgun. Get up."

She started to shake. "I think you're planning on shooting us both anyway. So if you want me up, step outside until I'm dressed."

He laughed, and with a sinking, terrified heart Martine became certain that none of her desperately sought bravado would have the least effect on him.

But then he moved. "Get dressed quickly. You're going to lead me to that gold. I know he had a map, and I know you can read it. Now move—and don't touch him. Not unless you want me to shoot him right now."

CHAPTER NINE

Kane could barely lie still and listen to Lander talk to Martine. It took more concentration and effort than anything he had ever done in his life.

But he didn't dare flinch or give any indication that he was conscious. Mentally he berated himself with a seething, helpless fury.

If only he hadn't been so damned *happy,* so convinced that he could free Nan from a lifetime of scorn, give her the righteousness she had craved, and at the same time keep his wife—the woman he had come to love so deeply that it had been agony.

Yeah, happy. He'd been so damned happy that he'd run around like an idiot, unaware of anything in the world except Martine and himself—and the sweet, sweet knowledge that despite it all, she loved him and at long last trusted him.

He should have known that Lander was coming. He should have been prepared to meet the man and protect his wife. Instead, he'd been compromised. Forced to listen while his precious and foolish little spitfire brazened it out on her own.

He knew her better than Lander did. He knew her almost as well as he knew himself. He heard the quiver in her words when she retorted to Lander's demands.

And when Lander walked away, he wanted to assure Martine. He couldn't. Not until he could get the shotgun away from Lander. He felt ill, when he thought of what a double-barreled shotgun could do to the human body. . . . Her body. Oh, God!

Kane remained still. He heard Martine stumble into her clothing and go to the entrance of the cave.

"Want some coffee, sweetheart?"

"Why not?" Martine replied with definite hostility.

Oh, love, play it cool, just for a few moments! Kane prayed silently.

Kane heard the dull clink of metal against plastic. "Thanks," Martine said dryly as she accepted coffee. There was a silence. Then she murmured, "How did you find out about the gold?"

"I knew about the old woman. When I recognized your husband, I put the family connection together on a hunch."

"How brilliant of you. What connection is that? And how did you recognize my husband?"

Lander started to laugh again. Kane groaned inwardly, clenching his teeth together to control the urge to ignore the shotgun and make a spring for his jugular.

"You still don't know who your old man is, do you, Martie? Well, I'll tell you then. Mr. Macho's the son of one of the richest cattle ranchers in Arizona. Of course, that isn't really his claim to fame. No, Golden Boy there started out by being some kind of war hero. Then he came home and started out on his own, digging for oil. Golden Boy had the Midas touch all right. He came up with black gold in some godforsaken dust bowl out in Texas. But of course, that wasn't enough for Mr. Marvelous. He happened to be around when the vice president was talking to a cattlemen's association. Wouldn't you know it? There was a madman hanging around, and Golden Boy steps up to wrestle the gun out of his hand before the old guy could go pluey. That's what got his picture in the papers, even though he tried to keep the

175

publicity down. Because of the old woman, you know. Damned idiot! Golden Boy, that is. He'd do just about anything to protect the old woman."

"Why?" Martine asked. Kane could hear the confusion in her voice, the hurt and the amazement. Yet he had to be glad. As long as she could keep Lander talking, they were doing all right. He could wait for his opportunity.

"I'll be damned!" Lander said. "Missy Martie, living in a fog at last! You haven't made the connection yet, have you? Listen up, stupid. The first Montgomerys to come out here were two brothers who came west just before the turn of the century. One moved to Tucson, married a society belle, and settled down to get rich on ranching. The other turned to prospecting and found quite a haul. But passing through these parts, he made a hell of a mistake for a man at that time. He fell in love with an Indian squaw and claimed to have married her. That Montgomery was some kind of a pal to your grandpa, Martine. Evidently he was going home to Tucson to pave the way to bring his bride home. Only he never made it. He was bushwhacked along the way. You gettin' all this, Martie?"

"I think so. Go on."

"Well, nobody wanted to believe the Apache girl. The whites rejected her, and so did her own kind—especially when she had a baby, being unwed and all that. Hell of a disgrace back then, you know. Almost as bad as a cocky little bitch who sleeps with her foreman, you know what I mean?"

Kane was stunned by the cool vehemence of Martine's expletive. Despite it all, he couldn't help smiling slightly. Bitterly. Tensely. The situation was still too uncertain for any real humor.

Lander laughed. "You understand what's going on yet?"

"Yes, I think so. The woman spent her life living alone,

content with her own knowledge that her husband had loved her. And—"

"No, you still haven't got it. The living Montgomery brother came here to pick up the baby, a little girl. She was raised with the white folk and grew up to a decent enough match."

"Lisa's parents?"

"Right as rain, Martie. You don't think Golden Boy came from the tarnished side of the family, do you?"

"I think he probably earned everything he got," Martine said smoothly. "But I'm still a little lost. And you seem to know everything. Go on."

"One more minute, lady. Then you're going to lead me to the gold. All right. The squaw always said she could prove she was Mrs. Montgomery if she ever saw any reason to do it. For years and years and years I guess she didn't. Then along comes her little granddaughter, hankering to marry into another of them uppity French families who just don't cotton to black sheeps in the family. She starts crying to her grandma, and wouldn't you know, Granny comes up with the map. Golden Boy is called in to do the dirty work. Only Grandma's so sick of notoriety that she makes him swear he won't breathe a word of what he's doing unless he finds the gold."

Kane could almost see Martine shaking her head.

"I don't understand. How does the gold prove anything?"

Lander chuckled deeply. "Martie, *I'm* after the gold. The Montgomerys are after what's supposedly buried *with* the gold."

"Which is?"

"The marriage license."

"Oh . . ." Martine breathed out softly.

Kane bit his lower lip, wishing that he could go to her, that he could explain why he had promised he wouldn't let anything out about Nan unless he could prove she had been legally wed all those years ago. He wanted to tell her that Nan had suffered enough, that in her old age she simply hadn't deserved any more heartache unless she could be vindicated. . . .

He couldn't explain anything now. He would be lucky to keep them both alive.

"So how did you find out about the gold?" Martie asked.

"Ah! Because I paid attention to local legend. I wasn't a rich kid, growing up with a silver spoon in my mouth."

"No, I guess not. And you were never willing to work to be rich, were you? You got wind of the general area and started digging up here before Kane did. You tried to kill Ed Rice when he came too close, didn't you?"

"Very smart, Martine. Too smart. Now, where's the map?"

"I don't know."

"I'll go in there and kill Lover Boy right before your eyes, Martie. And I'd rather not hurry. I want to see just how far you're willing to go to see him live."

"What if I help you find the gold? Will you leave us alone?"

"It's a hope, isn't it? Get the map."

"I'm really not sure where he keeps it."

"You'd better be."

Kane could hear Martine fumbling through their things. She took as long as she could, he realized. But then she hadn't known that it was in the food bag. He'd never thought to tell her. He knew where he was hunting.

And the pity of it was that he hadn't believed that the gold existed anymore. He dug where it should have been.

"Okay, Martie. You look at that map. And you tell me where the gold is. I know that you know, just like you know this place like the back of your hand."

"I—I really don't know. Not exactly. We've been digging for two days and haven't come up with anything. I mean, look for yourself. It should be in the back there, and we've already tried, as you can see."

Bless her heart, Kane thought. She couldn't know what she was doing, yet she was leading Lander on perfectly. Once they were past him, he could spring from behind. . . .

They walked on by. Silently Kane twisted around, watching the two at the back of the cave. He winced; Lander had the barrel of the gun dangerously close to Martine.

But Kane had to take a chance. He was certain that Lander didn't intend to leave any witnesses around.

He sprang to the balls of his feet, then shot out at Lander with all his strength. Martine screamed; Kane charged Lander, throwing him off-balance.

The shotgun went off. Blinding pain exploded in Kane's shoulder as the shot grazed him.

But he was on Lander. The blond man was fighting with a strength Kane wouldn't have expected, and the earlier blow to his head and the raze of his shoulder were dearly costing him power. They rolled across the cave floor together.

"No!" Martine screamed again.

"Get the hell away!" Kane shouted. Lander had his hands around Kane's throat. Kane rolled to dislodge him, his heart sinking.

Martine wasn't going to run! She was dancing around the two of them—trying to find the shotgun, he realized. Where the hell had it gone? Down one of the holes he had been digging probably.

God, his strength was going! He couldn't lose this fight. If he did, Lander would go for Martine. . . .

With a wild grunt he forced himself and Lander to start rolling again. Rolling and rolling with such an impetus that they were out of the cave and out by the boul-

179

ders. If he could just get Lander over by the straggling trees that grew between the rocks. . . .

He was blacking out, fading in and out of consciousness within split seconds. Lander slammed an elbow against his throat. Kane had to roll again, had to roll and manage to stand and lure Lander along.

The sunlight seemed incredibly bright, blinding, but the trees were coming into sight.

With a grunt and a desperate effort Kane caught Lander with a hard blow against the gut. Momentarily Lander weakened. Kane struggled to his feet, fighting the blackness that threatened to overwhelm him. "Come on, Lander, come on!" he roared to his opponent, backing away. Carefully, very carefully.

Lander came after him. And just when Kane thought he himself was going to fall, Lander let out a scream and fell into the ground. Rocks and dead branches cascaded down into the pit with him.

Kane sank down to his knees, catching his head between his hands.

And just at that moment Martine came charging out of the cliff, the shotgun raised in her hands, fire and tears in her eyes.

Slowly she lowered the shotgun. "Kane?"

"It's all right, my love."

"Where is he?"

Kane actually managed a smile. "I told you I was up here setting a trap for the mountain lion that day you came out and found me. I was really digging a trap. I just happened to be doing other digging at the same time," he added ruefully.

"Oh," Martine said weakly. She swallowed. "Is he—still alive?"

"Oh, I imagine. He's probably just a little scratched up."

"Oh, Kane!" she cried then. "You're bleeding all over the place. Oh, dear God!"

He saw her racing toward him. "The hole!" he shouted.

She stopped just in the nick of time. He smiled again. The world was going black, except for the pastel beauty of her face, that fiery splendor of her hair, the bright emerald glory of her eyes.

He pitched over onto his face.

Kane awoke with a dull pounding in his head. His fingers edged over something clean and fresh, and he slowly opened his eyes.

Despite that hammering pain, he awoke smiling—ruefully. Martie was sitting at his side, in her bedroom—their bedroom—watching him anxiously. He must look like a real fool, he thought, but it didn't matter a hell of a lot. Because he couldn't help it. He thought that everything was going to be all right, but he was scared. Scared with a sensation that riddled his gut with greater agony than that in either his head or his shoulder.

"We're home?" he asked.

She nodded, smiling, and reached out to touch his cheek tenderly. "You okay?"

"Well, I can see you, and I think that's all I really need."

"Oh, Kane."

"How did we get here?"

"I didn't know what to do. I couldn't lift you and I was scared to death even to glance at Lander. I got into the truck, and I think I could have made the finals for the Indianapolis Five Hundred on my way back to the ranch." She smiled. "Luckily my hands are getting accustomed to me behaving erratically. They didn't have me committed. Jim and Bill returned with me right away while Sonia called the doctor and the sheriff. They got

181

you into the bed of the truck. The doctor said that you should go to the hospital. I swore that I'd watch you like a hawk. The wound in your shoulder is clean, and he says he's convinced that you have a head like a rock. I agreed with him."

"Oh, you did, did you?" Kane asked.

Martine smiled and nodded pertly. "How do you feel?"

"Inept," he said dryly. "Some hero in the saddle, huh? I pass out cold on you."

She laughed delightedly. "Only after you'd clobbered the bad guy, Kane." Then her smile faded and she looked anxious—beautifully anxious. She started to lean against him, then pulled back as if she were afraid she would hurt him. Ignoring the pain in his arm, Kane reached out to pull her down to him.

"Oh, my God, do I love you!" he whispered.

She pulled away slightly, determined to see his eyes. "Do you really, Kane? I mean, can you really? I knew you had to be more than a drifter, but—"

"I wasn't anything but a drifter," he told her, "not until I met you."

"And you really fell in love with me?"

"Completely. Irrevocably. How could you ever doubt that? Never mind!" he answered his own question a little painfully. "Ah, Martine, I'm sorry! I did have to kind of trick my way onto the Four-Leaf Clover. Joe told me that Ed Rice was laid up. He was so worried about you—right when I needed to get my hands on the ranch. It didn't occur to me at first that Lander knew about the gold, just like he didn't know who I was at first. Not until he started putting things together. I wanted to tell you everything. But how could I convince you that I loved you and then turn around and admit that I had originally come here because of the ranch? And then there was Nan. . . . I can't tell you how wonderful a woman she is. She spent her youth as the subject of cruel notoriety. It wasn't until the forties that people seemed to forget about her and let her live in peace. She's old, Martine. If she winds up in the headlines again, it has to be for good reasons. Can you understand any of this? Why I had to ask you to trust me?"

"I was awful," Martine said.

"No, you weren't. I asked more of you than a man has a right to ask of any woman."

"I admit you have a rotten temper!" Martine laughed.

He caught her arms and swallowed. "I'm sorry about that, too, Martine. I jumped at you because I was scared. I was in the wrong—and I desperately didn't want to lose you."

"Kane," she said very softly, "I was wrong. I loved you enough to marry you. That should have meant that I loved you enough to trust you."

He smiled at her. There really wasn't a right or wrong answer to their past.

"Think we can start over?" he asked wistfully. "Forget the past?"

"I don't want to forget a minute of it," she whispered. "There was a lot of uncertainty, but there was also a lot of wonderful good that I intend to cherish all my life."

"I'll cherish you all my life," he said huskily.

Martine leaned down and kissed him, slowly and carefully but lingeringly. He tasted the sweetness of her breath, inhaled her scent, and felt surrounded by ambrosia.

"All our lives . . ." she whispered in awe.

"Lie down beside me," he said entreatingly.

"But your shoulder—"

"I have two sides, you know."

"Mmm," she said. "Your sweet one and your temperamental one!"

"Ouch!"

"It's true."

"No—I mean I know that. I have to move here a little bit."

"No, I'll move—"

"Don't you dare!"

Martine giggled but remained obediently where she was, snuggled against his good shoulder.

"Are we really disgustingly rich?" she asked.

"Well not 'disgustingly,' I hope."

"Oil wells?"

"Yeah, a few."

"Do you really think your family will like me?"

"They'll love you—not that it would matter in the least. No, I take that back. I love my family, even a little rascal like Lisa. I can't believe you thought I was having an affair with the torment of my youth!"

"She's a very pretty young woman!" Martine protested.

"Yes, I suppose she is," Kane said soberly. "But all this started because she wants to marry a snob."

"Maybe she won't marry him after all."

"Maybe not. But she's over twenty-one. I can advise her, but I can't run her life." He was very still for a moment. Then he sighed. "And it's all been for nothing. Lander will have to go on trial. Nan will wind up in the newspapers again, the old scandal all revived. For nothing. I know I've looked in the right place, but the gold just isn't there. Neither is the marriage license."

"Oh!" Martine cried, springing up in the bed.

"Have a heart!" Kane begged her, wincing as her sudden movement sent pain shooting through him again.

"I'm sorry, Kane, really I am."

"I know you owe me a few, but really, woman! Remember that you're my wife!"

Giggling, Martine planted a kiss against his throat. "I owe you lots and lots, but I think I have the best thing in the world to pay you back!"

He raised a brow. "Arsenic?"

"No. I'll be right back," she said mischievously.

When she disappeared through the doorway, Kane closed his eyes, smiling. She loved him. She had trusted him, and now everything was out in the open. They were alive, and in a few days' time he'd feel fit as a fiddle again and—

She really did love him. Completely. As soon as he could get up and about they would go to Tucson. He wanted his parents to know her; he wanted her to know the family. They all were such giving people. . . . They wouldn't stay long in Tucson, though. Not this time. He wanted a real honeymoon. Three weeks, a month maybe, to do nothing but play, get to know each other and talk until everything could be said; to sit in silence, happy just to be together.

"My wedding present, Mr. Montgomery!"

He opened his eyes. Martine was back in the room, standing over him with her head slightly cocked, her eyes gleaming like a thousand verdent fields. There was a worn leather folder in her hands. No, it was a buckskin folder.

"What is it?" he asked.

"Nan's marriage license," she told him huskily. "Well, I guess it's Nan's. Her name is different."

"Wildflower," Kane murmured incredulously.

"Yes, Wildflower. The English equivalent of her Apache name. Anyway, it's there. Very legal. She married Hugh Montgomery on December first, 1915."

"How . . ." Frowning, Kane looked up at his wife.

"I found the gold the day before you kidnapped me," Martine explained pertly.

"You found it?"

"Well, of course. I know the place very well, you know."

Kane started to laugh, except that laughing hurt, so he

made himself stop. "You let me do all that digging and sweating and picking when you'd already found the gold?"

"Well, I hadn't decided to trust you yet. For all I knew, I might have married a criminal. Besides, I liked to watch you dig. You have very sexy arms."

"Do I?"

"Yeah. And the rest of you is all right too."

Kane stared down at the paper in his hands, and a slow grin split his features.

"You're pretty all right yourself, Mrs. Montgomery," he murmured softly. "I think I like watching you in the shower best. Of course, I never got to see you dig, so I can't be sure."

Martine lay down beside him again, very carefully. "Do you know what I'll never, ever forget?" she asked seriously.

"What's that?"

"How you rode into my life with the sunrise," she whispered. "Just like the cavalry at the moment of distress. I'll never forget looking up and seeing you there. . . ."

He forgot all about his shoulder and his head and leaned over to kiss her; long, leisurely, with all his heart and soul.

At last he rose above her. "Does that mean that we can ride into the sunset together?" he asked huskily.

"Sunrise, sunset—any way you want to go," she told him.

"I love you, lady," he told her.

She smiled contentedly. It was true. Incredibly he had ridden into her life.

But even more incredibly he had ridden in to stay.

Fans of
Heather Graham
will delight in her boldest romance to date!

Golden Surrender

    Against her will, Ireland's Princess Erin is married off by her father to her sworn enemy, Prince Olaf of Norway. A Viking warrior, Olaf and his forces are needed by the High King to defeat the invading Danes.

    Nevertheless, the proud princess vows that her heart and soul will never belong to her husband, although her body might. Until one day that body, together with the life of her young baby, is almost destroyed by the evil Danes. When her husband *proves* his deep and abiding love for Erin by braving a desperate rescue attempt, she is forced to admit that her heart also holds a fierce love for her brave husband. $3.50   12973-7-33

Don't forget Candlelight Ecstasies and Supremes for Heather Graham's other romances!

THE SOUNDWORKS, INC.
Dept. DEL-125
P.O. Box 75890
Washington, D.C. 20013-5890

Please send me_____copies of THE BRIDGE ACROSS
FOREVER, a 4-cassette edition for $21.95.

☐ I have enclosed my check or money order for $_____
 ($21.95 for each 4-cassette edition)

☐ Please charge to ☐MasterCard ☐VISA

Card # ☐☐☐☐ ☐☐☐ ☐☐☐ ☐☐☐

Expiration Date _____

Signature _____
 (must accompany credit card orders)

Telephone # for charge sales: _____

Bank # _____
 (MasterCard only)

Ms./Mrs./Mr. _____

Address _____

City _____

State _____ Zip _____

Delivery within 3-4 weeks.

CALL TOLL FREE: 1-800-422-0111 and ask for Terry Dell.